# Liliane

## *Resurrection of the Daughter*

## Ntozake Shange

*Picador USA*
*New York*

...ed in this book are fictitious, ...idental.



*Design by Jaye Zimet*

*Library of Congress Cataloging-in-Publication Data*

*Shange, Ntozake.*
*Liliane / Ntozake Shange.*
*p. cm.*
*ISBN 0-312-13559-9*
*1. Afro-American women artists—New York (N.Y.)—Fiction. 2. Psychotherapist and patient—New York (N.Y.)—Fiction. 3. Young women—New York (N.Y.)—Fiction. 4. Afro-Americans—Mississippi—Fiction. 5. Queens (New York, N.Y.)—Fiction. I. Title.*
*PS3569.H3324L55 1995*
*813'.54—dc20* *95-21740*
*CIP*

*First published in the United States by St. Martin's Press*

*10 9 8 7 6 5 4 3 2*

*With love for my remarkable*
*father, Paul T. Williams, M.D.,*
*who lived in the spirit*
*& dignity of our people.*

# *Contents*

# *Acknowledgments*

The thanks and credit I must give to the incredibly mindful and emphatic people who assisted, encouraged, endured, and provoked me during the writing of *Liliane* is almost overwhelming. First, I want to thank Frank Stewart and Halima Taha as well as Irma and Miguel Algarin for providing hearth and home while I was on the road and inspiration when I was in New York. Then, too, Adal Maldonado, Mickey Davidson, Rasul Siddiq, Billy "Spaceman" Patterson, Jr., Jean-Paul Bourrelly, Candace Hill-Montgomery, and Gary Moore for repeated intense excursions into the worlds of these characters on stage, in rehearsal, or in the studio. The studied remarks of art historians Leslie King-Hammonds and Kathleen Coleman were of great significance to me. Finally, for rhythm and blues musicology, many thanks to Robert LaPierre and Donald Vereen.

Later in the process, but no less important, are the many

friends and colleagues in the theater who allowed me space and actors to actually "hear" those characters' voices and rhythms. Sydne Mahone, literary manager at Crossroads Theatre, Stanley Williams, artistic director of Lorraine Hansberry Theatre, Shelby Jiggetts, literary manager at the Public Theatre, and Walter Dallas, artistic director of Freedom Theatre, have contributed immensely to the breadth and specificity of this work under the auspices of the Lila Wallace Reader's Digest Foundation.

The prodigious efforts of Joycelyn Janck-Black in the preparation of this manuscript cannot be underestimated or overappreciated. The continuing support of my agents, Miriam Altshuler, Tim Seldes, and Joe Regal, has given me courage and reinforced my will to deliver lyricism with the truth. Finally, the patience and delight with which my editor, Michael Denneny, and his assistants, Keith Kahla and John Clark, met each chapter have been eminently sustaining.

Finally, I want to let someone know how open and eager my family, especially Savannah, Eloise, and Damani, have been for me to explore and bask in the arenas these characters offered me. But that's not quite true, because I cannot look at what has been accomplished here without acknowledging the work and counsel of Anthony Molino.

—NTOZAKE SHANGE
11 Marzo 1994
Olde City
Philadelphia

*Liliane*

# Room in the Dark

# I

———

———

——— Maybe it's not the silences.

———

——— Not the silences that bother me.

———

——— It's just the noise like a roar inside my head takes over when it's silent.

———

——— It's not quiet that I avoid. I never really talk out loud, *en pleine aire,* when I walk and I walk everywhere I can. I even prefer men who like to walk cause then we can talk with our eyes or our bodies or some strange sign'll bring us together. No. It's not quiet that I avoid. I'm quiet when I can hear music.

——— What music?

——— Oh, Bartók and B.B. King, Celia Cruz or Gloria Lynne. I don't like listenin' to ex-lovers very much, but I won't turn them off. Down maybe, but not off.

——— Are ex-lovers part of the noise in your head?

———

——— Or more in the silence?

——— You are interfering with my paradigm here. The music was part of a quiet that's quite appropriate and tangible, some pleasing part of my own body, my smile, my breath.

——— But you turn ex-lovers down.

——— Yes, down, not off. If I turned them off, they'd be part of the silence and then I wouldn't be able to hear anything palpable. It's like going to the moon.

——— The moon?

——— *Sí, la luna, la lune,* the moon in quiet with Machito or Turrentine is a sultry wanton giggle in my eye, but in silence the moon is just another dry, cracking surface like talkin' to white people all the time makes me choke, I can't breathe in silence.

——— Why is that?

——— Cause it presses down on me like a man who doesn't know his own weight can fuck me to death cause literally he's also blocking my esophagus, or like a wrong turn in the middle of the night in

South Boston can take my breath away. What difference does it make? It's quiet. It's silent. So what? You know, that's not my biggest problem right now.

——— What is your biggest problem?

——— Damn it. I told you, Jesus Christ, I musta told you a thousand times, I can't breathe.

——— When it's silent?

——— Yes.

——— That's why my silences, here with you, are troubling, then?

——— Oh . . .

———

——— How're you gonna help me in silence?

——— Well, then we can get to hear the noises in your head that are choking you.

———

———

——— It wasn't always true.

———

——— Uhmn. I didn't always need to hear anything or not hear anything. I have never had asthma, but now when somebody, even a soap starlet's voice isn't audible, if there's no music or chatter, or the phone's not ringing, I mean, not answered, I start gaspin' and next thing I know I'm holdin' my throat like my hands are healin' hands and I can't find any air. I forget where I am. My feet aren't really on the ground. Oh hell, I don't know where my feet are when there's that kinda force, my God, all I can imagine is being caught inside a roll of thunder. Now, could you get a holda yourself in a roll of thunder?

——— Why not lightning?

——— Cause I'm not burnin' up, I'm chokin' to death.

———

——— I told you I can't take this. I cannot survive in silence.

——— It's not really the silence you believe you can't survive. It's the noise in your head that you only hear in silence.

——— I've only mastered Quiet Time, how's that?

——— A start.

———

———

——— When it's really silent, I can't feel anything. I mean, I start to lose where the floor is. Why a flower is different from a rug, you know to feel, or even that walls don't curve under themselves like cats. I just know that I've gotta go to sleep right now or get outta here. I've gotta find somebody to talk to me. Somebody who knows me.

——— Somebody who loves you.

——— No.

——— No?

——— Doesn't matter long as he won't hurt me.

——— "He"?

——— Oh. Don't put on so. . . . You know, the bastard tried to choke me right at Sheridan Square the night my show opened. He spit on the sidewalk, turned round, and wrapped his fingers bout my neck like I was a magnum of Perrier & Jouët.

———

——— I thought . . .

———

——— We were lovers.

———

——— We usedta walk all the time and hear the most beautiful music.

———

——— Now, whenever a melody ends, I feel his fingers on my throat. Some of my hair in the back is caught in his fingers and he's shakin' me down from the Riviera as if nobody was around. People walked past, went across the street to the park. And nobody said anything. Did anything. The traffic kept comin', cars to New Jersey and cabs with medallions kept movin'. I heard the downtown IRT and all. Outta nowhere but he was right there. Outta nowhere I heard him screamin', "Who do you think you are?" and . . . I couldn't breathe. So I couldn't answer . . . I couldn't answer. . . .

———

——— It's me, Lili . . . it's just me. . . .

———

———

——— This is very important.
——— Yeah. How's that?
——— Well. You turn down ex-lovers in quiet.
——— Yeah, I'm not afraid in music.

——— Or language.

———

——— It's these silences.

——— Where lovers become assassins without warning. It's the noise. A horrible throbbin' roar . . . and . . .

——— You can't hear yourself.

———

——— Or protect yourself.

——— I can't even say my name. I cannot breathe.

———

——— But why, why would he hurt me like that?

——— Maybe, he couldn't stand to hear the music in you.

——— Music? Oh God. He even shouted when he talked about music he loved, like a delicacy in the tone of his voice would actually impugn the virility of a note. . . . I like to caress sounds and images I care for with my fingers, my tongue, my lips. He was always shouting, shouting til my ears hurt.

——— Noise, again. A noise that hurts, yes?

——— Why am I lowering my eyes, when you say that? "A noise that hurts."

——— It's the silence.

——— How can hurtin' be associated with shame? Lowering my eyes cause somebody's hurt me, then, I'm guilty of . . . feelin'? That's crazy.

——— Maybe. Maybe not. Could be protecting yourself from the Gorgon or Medusa. So you don't turn to stone and stop feeling.

———

——— You're not helpin' me when you don't respond.

——— I'm gettin' a knot in my throat. I'm frightened and my heart's beatin' up and out that window.

———

——— Don't you hear me talkin' to you, dammit?

——— Yes, I'm here. You are doing impressive work, Liliane.

———

——— We are starting to decipher the noise.

——— Oh, oh. My ears ache.

——— The noise.

——— Yes. Yes. He's screamin' and chucklin'. Please . . . I don't want to cry. I don't want to start cryin', talk to me, please.

——— He's always talking to you, even in the silence. Before I can really talk to you, we've got to hear what he is screaming at you. Then we can end this conversation with this man who can't caress words or images he cares about like you do.

——— There's a cave in my chest.

——— That's where his voice can boom and steal the air from you, so you can't breathe, Liliane.

——— Yes, I know.

——— Take those noises he makes of words and make them small enough for your mouth to say.

——— But it's so mean. Why say such mean things?

——— That's how he makes the silence into such a racket. When there is nothing, he's still there screaming, he's right there making sure it hurts.

——— I can't take this.

——— Then he's pretty well succeeded.

——— I could just keep talkin' . . . I could . . .

——— Lili, you don't have to keep hearing him, resounding when you are being still.

——— I do. I do, if there's no music.

———

——— But you said I had the music.

——— Yes.

——— You know it was sucha lovely night we went walkin' in Noe Valley. All the harbor, two of those bridges that hang in the night, glowin', like magic. I was feelin' pretty good. I'd made these labia outta different kinds of soil, you know, fertile, infertile, sandy, black, clay. Was feelin' sorta sexy and stretched in a good way. We're goin' down this hill and lights are twinklin', ordinary houses glistened like FAO Schwarz, lovely, you know. I'm plannin' this party, you know, to show my labia boxes . . . He starts laughin'.

———

———

——— What was so funny?

——— Well, he thought it was just hilarious that my artist friends, alla my artsy friends, had girlfriends who weren't black. Mingo's girl was Chinese. Jose-Albero had Myo who was Vietnamese. Joe Scahenger had a white woman and, lemme see, I think, maybe it was Adam was with a Chicana from East Oakland.

——— What was so funny about that?

——— Well . . .

——— Yes.

——— Uh. He thought it was so funny. For all the labia boxes I made it didn't look like there were many men sniffin' after a colored woman. Thought niggahs weren't so revved up bout white women no more, they sure weren't comin' home to get none. "Looks like don't nobody want you all, English-speakin' Negresses." He kept laughin' . . . and I am havin' trouble breathin', now. See what you've done?

——— Yeah.

——— Well, what is that?

——— We broke the silence.

# Fawns of the Diaspora Court Liliane in Paris, While Tabou Combo Whispers "Coq Qualité" in Her Ears

The sunlight hit Jean-René. The sepia half-moon of a mole by his right cheekbone glistened, steaming coal in a fast car gliding through the hills of Morocco. We stopped to have a very French picnic: kisses. Shadows of lips and teeth against luxurious auburn soil. The sun always slipping in and out of the bends of limbs, wine from Lisbon dancing mouth to mouth, tongues tracing patterns of clouds, scents of goats, sheep, and the last of my Opium, somewhere near Meknes. I wanted to stay in Paris I'd thought, but no. He said he'd have to have me somewhere I'd never been. I'd laughed. I woke in Casablanca to morning prayers and croissants.

If only my mother could see me now: Jean-René meticulously placing strawberries, blueberries, kiwi, grapes, melon balls in a crescent round my vulva. Oh dear. Oh dear. Oh dear. My cat has yellow eyes. Now my pussy has lime-green ones, amber pupils, slits.

Casablanca was hot, noisy, trashy, roadblocks everywhere, the war in Spanish Sahara. We retreated like Anaïs to the countryside. This Guadaloupean velvet spur of a man and me, Liliane. I travel a lot. I look at men and take some home or leave the country, borders have never intimidated me. My passport is in order and I carry letters of credit, perfume, four fancy dresses and six nightgowns. I always sleep naked alone at least once a week. I pray and say hail marys by some window at dusk. It's always best for me to deal with the sacred when I'm naked. For me it has something to do with humility.

I found Jean-René eating souvlaki at the fast-food place next to the Moulin Rouge. I was flirting with some Brazilians from the Folies Bergères. I'd just left Lisbon, and Angola was on all our minds.

In my last paintings, before I left New York, I superimposed AK-47s over fetal transparencies under Frelimo banners. *La Luta Continua* was the name of the show. There was no way to stop my fingers, my arms, I was jumping up and down ladders to get the touches of blood and fresh corpses finely detailed so there'd be no doubt that the Portuguese left a country the way vampires leave blond white women: drained of life and scarred. I paint. I don't talk too much. The world overwhelms me. I can give up what I see. I see a lot. I believe in honor, color, and good sex.

Machado and Axel from the Folies were doing their best to entice me to La Plantation, an Antillean discotheque near St.-Germain-des-Près. I looked Jean-René in the eyes once and knew that would never happen. Why would I want to dance in a plantation anyway? Even in the presence of the singularly defined muscles of Latin dancers, one on either side, the man I was slowly seducing across the room just kept looking at me, knowing where I'd be going. I like that. I like a man to know what the deal is going to be in an instinctive, absolute, lyrically facile manner. I like a man with confidence. Take me from these two sweet muthafuckahs simply by looking. Do that and I'll be gone. Wherever we are going. I mean, if a man's up to that. I love double entendres, double negatives, duels. Some cocks have triggers; others are freckled or uncircumcised.

I decided I wanted some baklava. Right over there where the man with eyes was sucking me up. Imagine that, disappearing into a stranger's eyes in Paris. How would they find me? Who would know to look? I don't leave any tracks, am quick to burn bridges. My friends, well my friends, the real ones, wouldn't think twice. Liliane, she's having dessert. They'd smile, unless no drawings arrived in say a month or two. That is my signature, after all, an image. I forget what I was wearing that night. Probably the floor-length azure crepe with lace triangles up to my hips and no back at all. I like that dress, but I'm going to dye it *grise: ma robe grise.* Oh, Jean-René slid his eyes into my mouth and asked me if I had plans for the evening. *"Mais non, monsieur, j'ai pensé que tu voudrais faire des arrangements."* I told him my name several hours later. By then he could barely speak.

Jean-René with the black nipples that grew. Each tongue flick drawing black licorice sticks tiptoeing over my teeth and tongue. Third World delicacies. Cascades of caviar round my neck. *Noire et blanche.* He played the piano, when he wasn't near me. Actually he was a concert pianist. He played Bach and

Stravinsky, when he wasn't near me. He sometimes played scales, but anybody can do that.

Coming down the Champs-Élysées all the record stores blasted Stevie Wonder's newest release, *Songs in the Key of Life*. "Isn't She Lovely" chased me from corner to corner. I didn't know if I should hide near the grated windows or fly through the night like some paradisiacal bird of color: many colors. Any color, everything matches: spirit; free spirits; about to be in love a lot. Stevie Wonder pushing us closer together. Eventually, I stopped running. I walked fast. Waited by the curb. At some point he put his arm over my bare shoulder. His fingers grasped my skin so there were five imprints. A woman with three sets of fingerprints. That would drive Interpol crazy. I was already grazing the edges. I didn't leave his side til we got to where we began. Remember, the hillside outside Meknes? You won't believe me, but I heard Charlie Palmieri in Paris on our way to heaven. Those fingers again. I'll have to draw it for you, okay?

Such character you'd expect from Cecil Taylor's fingers, or my grandfather's, Frank, who was a master carpenter. My fingers still smack of perfumed talcum, white gloves, and honeyed lotions. My calluses are elusive, if ever present, closer to my heart than my wrists which are deceitfully delicate. Veins, blue-black pulsing, rise eloquently from Jean-René's hands, small muscles throb over the white and black keyboard, eliciting the reveries of Bartók, Monk, Abrams, and Joplin. My back refused to sound anyone but Satie, Bobby Timmons, and John Hicks. This frustrates Jean-René. When he smacks my cheek with the back of his hand, only Andrew Cyrille comes to mind. The Frenchman is unnerved. The music of my body is deliberate. There's nothing I can do about how I sound. When I open my mouth, Shirley

Cesaire and Jeanne Lee scramble for the skies, my tongue finds his somewhere high above the treble clef. We're pulled back, flat to the soil. Sun running us pianissimo while our sweat moistens the virginal African grass. Our bodies lay claim to the earth, silhouettes of lovers, smooth unbroken lines, enveloped by tall brush, quivering in the wind, as tongues would wag in whatever language were our license with each other known beyond this side of the road. Meknes.

I want to paint now. Throw Jean-René's swarthy limbs over the pillows I laced with scents of raspberry, bay leaves, cinnamon. He'll rest in soft fragrances: me and my spices. I pull out my brushes and pastels. Sequester myself on a rocky cliff before the walled village. Women wrapped in blue-black swishes of spun cotton float through the streets. The men in white and tanned robes saunter with a holy gait toward a precipice. It is dusk. I am using wine as water to moisten my paints. The air is too light for oils. Watercolors, moistened pastels alone, capture the haunting prayers of these disciples of Allah. I am allowing my fingers to float as the women do, over the cobblestones, reddened dirt paths, billows of dust following donkeys, mules, bicycles. My brush strokes unevenly. The abyss around which we assemble in honor of Allah. The evening prayers begin. The sun splits open, cries for atonement and adoration pierce the clouds, hovering weights above our heads. I feel a sharp pain in my groin, my heart is racing, I am losing my breath. I see Jean-René. His eyes are glazed over as if in a trance. I swoon. My blood has come. The forces of this sacred earth have drawn menses from my body. The sun sets. I use this last scarlet liquid to highlight the figures in my painting. Hundreds of women, floating blue-black apparitions etched *rouge,* the soil *rouge,* the brush-colored caftans of the men dragging in blood. The Jihad has simple implications. Holy war. Where is there war without blood. Blood falling to the ground. I am weak now. I leave my paints and brushes alone, slide over to Jean-René, who holds me close to him as if we'd been in danger, as if communion with God was a travesty. We can't kiss, not now. Fierce angels are everywhere, sneering and eager to mock our frailties. Mortals, flesh, driven souls, seeking wholeness with mouths, fingers, wrapping limb over limb to become one. Music issuing forth from their depths, entering one another, desperately seeking that one song, one melody of peace. The angels gather above the rushes, snide, shaking their heads, wagging their fingers through the air, lighting up the sky and calling thunderous rhythms to startle us, to insist we acknowledge our nakedness. I pull my paintings to me. The colors pour onto my skin. I am now streaked blue-black, reds, yellow, luminous blue. Jean-René grabs my hand. I hold my paintings, soaking in the downpour. Scarlet drops fall from my bosom to my toes, to the soil, blue-black smudges crowd off my own sepia tones. Lurching toward the car, I turn. Drop the paintings. Fall on my knees, bleeding. Pleading with Allah to bless me, to accept me as an instrument of the holy spirit. Jean-René whispers hail marys in my ears. I am digging for the scent of my god. My hands are covered with small rocks, brown mud and slivers of brush up to my wrists where the clay has dried like bracelets. Jean-René lifts me in one moment, holding me a statue over the ruins of my art.

My hands were small fists, knotted round the earth I'd gathered. Jean-René glanced at me once. "We're going to Fez. If you want to save that dirt, there's a small box in the back. Wipe the blood from your arms and face or we'll never get a hotel room." My eyes followed the rise of his cheekbones, the arrogance of his slender nose, and the flippant curve of his lips, those finely wrought muscles in his forearm. Yes, the box, save the soil for earth paintings. Wipe the blood away. Watch Jean-René take the road, soaring, an ebony eagle, round mimosa and hibiscus and palms. Jean-René smoldering like Mont St. Pierre, but this volcano was holding the eruption for me. The woman shedding blood and soil in the backseat of an Antillean eagle's flight to Fez.

I liked to kiss Jean-René on curves or steep downhill glides. I liked the wandering tree limbs to let their shadows enter his mouth as my tongue did. Shadows and tongue skipping and sliding over his pearl teeth and blackberry lips. Dangerous, you say? *Mais non.* You're talking to the woman who was physically searched three times at Kennedy Airport because the buzzer went off whenever I went through the screening device. I had forgotten to take my ben-wa balls out. They're no threat to international security. When they're working, the last thought on my mind is hijacking a plane. Why should I swipe an airplane when young Guadeloupean peacocks stalk about Paris and fly me to Morocco in the middle of the night. All he needs is a piano and me. I carry my own entertainment: color, wine, brushes, pencils. My ben-wa balls attracted no attention at Orly Airport. I guess they could see the contentment of my face, or smell my pleasure. I always assume people can smell how happy I am, how full of love I can be. That's how Jean-René found me in Paris at that fast-food souvlaki place. He could smell my joy, he said. I told him I heard Eric Dolphy in his eyes.

# Room in the Dark II

——— The distance is not really so great.
——— But that's Brooklyn.
——— And . . .
——— You think he goes there on purpose?
——— He lives there, you say.
——— Right.
———
——— Well, I guess, that's the end of that.
——— Yet, you have no problem going to Montreal, Paris, and you feel Brooklyn is too far away.
——— It's not there.
———
———
——— Brooklyn is not there?
——— No, it's just the bridge.

——— What bridge?
——— Well, how many do you know about?
——— The Bay Bridge, the Chesapeake Bay Bridge, the Verrazano-Narrows Bridge, le Pont-Royal . . .
——— So now we're *"sur le pont d'Avignon."* [They sing together.]
———
——— If you gonna sing it like that won't nobody find it. Avignon'll disappear from history you sing like that.
——— How does it go?
——— What?
——— The bridge?
——— The bridge? Went somewhere with Art Blakey. You can't hear it?
——— Not the way you do.
——— That's funny. Nobody hears anything like anybody else does, but we manage to talk and sing. We were singing, we were, weren't we? In the fall Daddy came in one evening when the sky looked most on fire. It was World Series time. The garden lost all the sunlight every afternoon when swarms of birds black as, black as the Magi rolled up, kept the whole house in a . . . in an embrace, like we didn't belong in the rest of the world at all. And it was quiet. Mama was somewhere singing something nobody could hear. I sat by the window waiting for the shadows of the birds to float over me and the dead leaves, when this lush, wonderful warmth lifted me outta myself into the garden. I thought the sun had pushed the birds out the way, but it was

Daddy playin' Art Blakey and the Jazz Messengers. I thought it was illicit.

——— Why did you think that?

——— Oh my. Because, as Felipe says, "Jazz is a woman's tongue stuck, dead in your mouth."

——— Yes, that's what he thinks. What did you think?

——— Well, we awready established that you can't hear it.

——— What?

——— The bridge?

——— No.

———

——— But it was warm and lush.

——— Yes, yes it was.

———

——— You wanna know something funny. I had this dream. I was at a truly elegant party. Parquet floors, crystal octagonal chandeliers, and singing champagne glasses. Everything wonderful to taste. All the men in the world I ever dreamed about holding me: They were all there. I was having a wonderful time, sort of like Scarlett O'Hara at that first party at Seven Oaks. Well, I felt unbearably gorgeous, when suddenly I realized that my clit was glowing. I mean, like silver neon lights in Las Vegas, my pussy was beaming artificial light all over this very delicate and elegant fête. No matter how I held myself, what contortions I forced my body into. This glow was irrepressible. People started to stare at me. I was so embarrassed. Then, just as I was about to cry, he came in, took possession of the space, addressed the whole damn lot of them and said: "Oh, her clit's going to get brighter than that. We've been working on it."

———

——— God, that's funny.

——— Well, that accounts for your shoelaces.

——— What'd you mean?

——— They're silver lamé, no?

——— Well, yes, but I bought these the day after . . . oh, I get it. I'm wearin' my clit on my shoes.

——— No, more like the glow. The unbearably gorgeous glow you're wearing and getting around fairly well, I might add.

——— Yeah, right.

———

———

———

——— Did you ever hear that tune "Moanin," by Bobby Timmons?

——— I think, I can vaguely recall something like that.

——— I finally met him when he was playing in the cocktail lounge part of this jazz joint. What the fuck was he doin' there? I mean, Jesus, he was frail and so modest. I kept hearing him playin' and looking at him. It doesn't match.

———

——— The music and the man.

——— Not at all like your clit and your shoes.

——— I'm not kiddin'. It disturbed me. I kept hearin' those chords in the fall, when the birds go south, and Daddy comes home, and, then, this great, oooh, this great rush of sound takes over. It was Art Blakey. . . .

——— You said it was illicit?

——— It was dark. It was quiet.

———

——— You should talk. You live with your goddamned mother.

——— How do you know I live with my mother?

——— You called me from her house last night in my dream. You said it wasn't safe to do our work today. Communication lines were down. All the bridges were out.

# "I Usedta Drink, Smoke and Do the Hoochie-Koo," or What's a Girl to Do When Her Mother Looks Like Ruth Brown

"Is your mother a Communist, Liliane?" I asked the nicest way I could manage. I didn't know what she would say, or could say, for that matter. My mama was daylights different I should say, cause I was a gift or a trial come to her late in life. Sometimes, I thought Liliane's mama was more like us than Mama's mama, you know what I mean? Well, I am every bit the lady, but my curiosity had gotten the best of me. Liliane was truly tickled, I thought. She gazed over the Gulf waters with not a trace of chagrin or indignation.

"What would inspire you to say such a thing, Roxie? You can't possibly be a Communist and constantly talk about what's rightfully yours and the necessity of beauty and, what else, oh, the derelictions of the unrefined. Hell, no, she's not a Commie."

"But whenever we had to watch the McCarthy hearings she'd never let us talk or play. She was always making what I feel were very prejudiced remarks, whenever one of those stars from Hollywood took that amendment about his friends and such. I think I have every right to ask about your mother's leanings. The Negro can't be too careful about his friends. That's what my folks always say. Remember the unionists left us to our own means at the drop of a hat. Don't forget that."

Liliane threw a shell she'd been running along her limbs til millions of little goose bumps pushed hairs toward the sun. She was slower than me, I thought, and she's not even from the South. I asked a simple question and wanted a simple answer, not a complicated treatise. Her words floated in the gusts of wind on a slow journey to the welling surf.

"Roxie. The Civil War was before our time. There are Negroes dying and fighting right now. We were dying and fighting before Communists had a name for themselves, my dear."

"Don't you think I know that. I do believe my parents are descendants of bona-fide free. How could I not know the War was over." With that I was sure I'd sent Liliane's words clear to the Yucatán, or Cuba, maybe. Liliane's mama had been to Cuba. She'd been to the Tropicana where girls just like me and Liliane appeared from cypress and magnolia trees with macaw and peacock feathers framing their faces. Oh yes, maybe my words could be swept all the way to Havana and Fidel's lips. I wanted my syllables to change shape and sound, become some revolutionary kiss by the cheeks of Castro, but I couldn't tell Liliane, since her mama had shown us movies of her trip to Cuba last summer. Surely, a girl whose mama booed the McCarthy hearings, who wrote letters protesting the treatment of Paul Robeson, and went to Havana for vacation would understand how much I needed to win. I needed to see Negroes or mulattoes, bona-fide free, or somebody who looked like me win for a change.

I was too young to be so tired. I thought the Northerners were down here to help us cause they weren't worn down by white folks yet. Maybe that wasn't the truth, though. Where Liliane lived the crackers was just as evil as they could be. I'd a mind to ask Missus Lincoln if Liliane couldn't come on down and live with me, but my mama was so close to old, I knew better. But what I wanted Liliane to help me with was overwhelming me. I wanted to be, plain as that, just be, without all the planning, preening, fixing, and carrying on. You don't know what I am talking about, do you? All the polishing of Negro girls about to be grown is as clear as I can get. I was getting the brunt of it, myself. How to serve bouillon as opposed to gumbo. What fork goes where and why. When to take gloves off and when to put them on. I was weary, weary.

Liliane's mama didn't cotton to any of that. No, sir. Liliane had a mama who went her own way. I thought it was her name that freed her, Sunday Bliss. Liliane hooted like a low white to my mind, when I told her this. I wasn't allowed to hoot like that.

"S. Bliss Lincoln, Roxie, is hardly a woman who's thrown reason to the winds," Liliane explained casually. "Besides, she only tells special people like me and you what the 'S' stands for, says her name is what lets folks know she's a colored woman."

"Negro, Liliane, Negro. We don't have to say colored anymore." Sometimes for such a modern girl Liliane was caught in a mess of old-timey ways. "Negro is the word to use today, my papa insists on it. Less you want to do some very tedious chores, don't say that other appellation for our folks around here."

"Roxie, do you ever talk anything besides 'the War' and the race? Do you? There's so much more to life than what white folks have to do with. We can't spend our whole lives worrying ourselves about what they're going to do, what they think of us, or where they are hiding, for that matter."

"You can say that. Ku Kluxers aren't just around the bend from you."

"You know that for a fact, do you?" Liliane smiled at me the kind of smile I'd been taught accompanies a demure reply when a young man asks for a dance.

"Why, Liliane. You are fit on frustrating me this very moment, heifer."

We laughed and lay back on the rocks. The sand was so fine I sometimes thought it was more like another skin, hot and supple. I wondered did Liliane notice how peculiar and awkward people looked trying to walk on sand, sinking and stumbling, disrupting patterns in continuous motion, sacred doodles of the breeze, I thought. The sea was flirtatious that day, too. No signs of trouble, no torn tree limbs or perplexing bones. I saw my words on their way to Cuba, to fighters with Maceo, to the hands of Placido writing so long ago. Liliane thought I was parochial. That's what she called my "race" talk, but I'd been talking to the *black black bones* of dead slaves and freedmen since I was a child. My mama says I'm still a child. Shucks, she probably thinks Tallulah is a child. I can't find a way yet to tell anyone that I'm not a girl interested in the way things are or used to be. I am dreaming of what we'll be that's different, that'll set us aside, a generation that confounds white folks. But that doesn't mean I don't want to marry well.

"Liliane, don't you think it's amazing that your mama married well and doesn't go to meetings or balls or things? How do you think she managed that? Not coming to the Negro affairs with your daddy, I mean."

"You'll have to ask her," Liliane responded, handing me the cocoa butter for her back.

"You can use this on stretch marks, my mama says. That way your husband will stay nigh."

"Roxie, Negro women don't get stretch marks."

"You only say that because your mama is so young and pretty. I got a mama who is a Negro woman with stretch marks, so don't you tell me. I know what I'm talking about."

We were quiet for a while, I guess. I never understood why white folks claimed the slaves stood the heat so well God must have meant for us to pick cotton. I couldn't stand the heat. Liliane couldn't stand the sun directly on her face, either. She and her mama had masks they put on to bathe and lay out to tan. See, I really had to know more about Sunday Bliss. She was such a mystery to me. Liliane just knew her mama so I couldn't hold that against her. Yet, a mama who didn't receive visitors at every reception, gave mambo lessons, looked like Ruth Brown and grew orchids, when the rest of the world was losing its very mind, must have been wonderful. Must be wonderful. S. Bliss got on well with my folks. My mama's not an easy soul to know, either. On guard for enemies of the race at every moment, but she saw them in the strangest of quarters: the lawyer with bad diction, the model with a flat nose, the singer with too much jewelry. Why, once I actually told her that she was the cross the race had to bear. Oh my, what a conflagration fell upon us when I said that. Still, I want to marry well, steady like the sea rocking me on the sands that are my skin.

The lands that were once ours been eaten up by no good white assessors, poor crops, and fatigue. My papa skittered from New Orleans to Mobile, then Galveston to Montgomery aiding the plight of Negroes forced to defend themselves in white men's courts. That's how Liliane and I were in one another's company so much. The race actually threw us together. Our fathers were champions of the Negro civil rights, but mine was clearly less the rabble-rouser, more the old school, I mean. If Papa hadn't known when to push and when be still, I imagine I would be another dead Negro girl gone up in flames one night, while the townsfolk milled about, mourning our recklessness in the face of crackers crazed with hate. Defending the daughters of the South, how many times had I heard that? I was a daughter of the South, I thought to myself. Maybe I do understand more about S. Bliss Lincoln than I thought. I wanted to be like her, not like Liliane. S. Bliss, her laughter wrapped around us when she kissed us good night, the same as waves fold over themselves when the tide comes in.

"Liliane, are you sure your mother's not a Communist?" I didn't wait for an answer. I rolled over to dream where no other Negro girl had dared. Liliane took all sorts of things for granted. Not me, I know to cherish now. So many folks had been awready blown apart.

I go to church I could be so much blood-soaked cloud and dust, scraggly blackened wood beam smoldering in my glowing flesh, so many colored buds, colored blossoms, to be picked at by coroners, laughed at by crackers, reported in the news: "Pieces of young colored girls gathered today in a festival of death held from Mobile to Biloxi." My mama does get on me when I talk like this. "This ain't much of anything, child. Don't you know how much worse slavery times must have been?" "No, Mama. I don't know how much worse. I truly don't."

The sun was preening herself on the edges of the green-smoked seas by the time I roused myself. As always in my dreams I'd been to tea with Nicholás Guillén and Léon Dámas on a veranda that overlooked the port where no more slave ships arrived, no Spanish planters shouted orders for their porcelains to be treated delicately by slaves who'd have broken more than glass if given a chance; no young women caked white flour on their faces to be sure they weren't mistaken for quadroons or octaroons or, heaven forbid, a *mulatta.* No, none of them were romping in my dreams. No COLORED ONLY in Cuba. That's why my dreams went there. That's why I knew all this would end someday. First Haiti, then Cuba; could Mississippi be far behind? Liliane was incapable of ascertaining the ironies, of course. She loathed the separation required by law for drinking water and eating in public places, but I assured her this had no effect on us at all. "Liliane, we simply don't go there, any of those 'theres,' so how could I be in a frenzy about what I don't do." As you can guess, Liliane remained skeptical. Nevertheless, she's my friend. Her naïveté cannot hamper my devotion.

"Liliane, I do believe we should be getting home now. The sun's going down this very minute. We got to help Mama attend to her guests and get ready ourselves, you know. The big party for the Legal Defense Fund is this evening. Have you forgotten?"

"How could I forget that? Is it true Martin Luther King himself is coming?"

"Oh, I don't know. Nobody knows when he might be coming, but a lot of other teenagers our age will be around for sure. That's why we need to get back, tend to this hair and make ourselves beguiling. That's what I think."

"Roxie, this is hardly the time to be flirting with boys, when the race is at a crossroads. That's what my daddy says. The Negro race is at a crossroads no less daunting than the move to Emancipation. It's very serious." Liliane was becoming her more energetic self, wrestling with her hair and limbs like she could bring no order to bear upon them in the Gulf breeze that undid everyone's best intentions.

"Well, old slaves, abolitionists, and Negro cavalrymen had children. I don't see any reason civil rights attorneys shouldn't be procreating as well, and I intend to look presentable when I see them this evening. You suit yourself, but that beatnik attire will certainly seem out of place, if you ask me."

"There's nothing wrong with my turtlenecks and slacks. There's nothing sacred in dresses and slips, you know."

"If you insist on embarrassing your parents that way, make a point of using a whole lot of deodorant. That's what I'd do if I was you. Don't want to be stink and look like nothing as well."

"Roxie, my mama says if a boy can't see past what you're wearing, he'll certainly never know your true worth."

"Well, I guess, you could hope they see you at all."

"Oh, Roxie, you make me sick with this Scarlett O'Hara

mess." Liliane whipped our blanket through the air so the sand pricked me like so many hot combs.

"Liliane. Stop it. Stop it, this minute. I'll never get this stuff washed and pressed in time, if you don't just quit. Stop, now. Do you hear me?"

Liliane giggled irrepressibly, ran to the water's edge, and kept going. I wished for a minute the current would sweep her into Cuban waters where she'd see up close that revolutionaries have children, their beaches don't have COLORED ONLY signs, and the girls wear really pretty dresses, lipstick, and nail polish. But Liliane walked back from her brief swim, still laughing; she never got to Cuba.

My mama didn't need a bit of help from us. I could tell by the way she was sporting herself when we went in the back door. R. C. Golightly was every inch a lady of the house, if I must say so myself. I joked with my mama, that she must be named after the Royal Crown Cola people, but she said that was impossible cause as far as she knew Royal Crown Cola didn't have slaves. That was supposed to be a joke, but I know her name was short for Roman Catholic because her folks had taken up with the church shortly after Emancipation and credited the Pope with their freedom. It was so down-homey, I didn't care for that idea much. Plus, not a whole lot of the slaves were bamboozled by priests like my mama's folks, but R.C. was her name. That was my mama and she looked like all get out to my mind, old as she was. And she was old.

R.C. was in a forsythia-yellow cocktail dress that actually lit her up like the three o'clock sun. She was portly, but well shaped, and the softness of the cloth summoned even more graciousness from every gesture.

"You girls, run along now, company's coming. I know you must have your sights set on a fine time. So let's get going, you hear."

Liliane had never seen my mama so smart before. I knew from her face, blank like that, she just wasn't expecting such a transformation in R.C. Folks like to think little of my mama. She married late, somehow got hold of me, and my father was hardly a run-of-the-mill sort, always defending Negroes out of their place. But Papa just shook his head and tapped his pipe. "Our place is any place we choose," he said. And R.C. would run her hands by his whiskers and pull the funny end of his mustache: "You tell 'em, Daddy." Liliane's mother never touched her father as far as I could tell. S. Bliss just appeared to be doing what she was expected to be doing out of the blue. Liliane said that's cause her parents had an understanding that if you had to ask for something, it mustn't of been freely given and was, therefore, not worth having. I could never get to a clear comprehension of that reasoning, but I sometimes think all Northerners are simply quite eccentric.

Now, I'm not bragging or putting on airs or anything like that at all, but our house did seem grand. After all we'd just about turned spit to gold to keep it since Reconstruction times. One of my father's granddaddies had done well with the scalawags and carpetbaggers, who licensed general stores to him when it got too bad for white radicals to be seen with Negroes. So that great-granddaddy built himself a swear-for-Jesus plantation house in a small grove by the Biloxi town limits. That way, since we were unincorporated, the white folks couldn't tax us to oblivion when the mood suited them. Anyway, the place was just a dream to behold to my eyes. Mama had lights suspended through the cottonwoods. A dance floor of real heavy rubber was set out in the yard. Lawn tables were placed by the sides of the fences, so the roses and wisteria lingered over possible conversations. We were expecting a few white folks, cause the Legal Defense Fund was integrated, so things were a bit more dramatic than ordinarily before a party at my folks' place. Yet we'd had so many guests for a week, since Negroes couldn't stay in hotels nearby, that I felt very much at home, even though it wasn't quite like my home with so many grown folks, Liliane and her folks, my folks and me. Oh, what a wonderful way to end a week of planning and strategy for the Negro.

"Roxie, aren't you afraid here? I mean, living in Biloxi," Liliane asked me, while I was zipping up this sundress of pink and red flowers I'd finally convinced her to wear.

"No, not unduly," I replied. "Oh, oh, Liliane, you look delightful, I must say. Look at yourself." I moved her over to the wall mirror where Liliane smoothed her waist and pushed up her bosom how my mama did sometimes to no avail. "See there, just a darling you are."

"Thanks."

Liliane blushed, I swear. I knew once I got her in a dress she'd be more amenable to my suggestions. Liliane's personality changed, you see, when she was all gussied up. She was more like her mama, you see, when her beauty was undisturbed. I, myself, was in an A-line dress with a hint of bust: fuchsia, very good color for me.

"Roxie, this is Mississippi," Liliane blurted through the last shreds of light creeping round our window shades. So out of the mood, she was.

"Yes, Liliane, this is Mississippi. And we are the veritable belles of the ball," I retorted.

"Yes, indeed, you are. Both of you are looking lovely." In the doorway to my room stood none other than S. Bliss Lincoln herself. S. Bliss in an array of silk crepe that swept the floor as she walked toward us. She was Aphrodite, I thought. She must be Venus. Then I remembered Ruth Brown, when S. Bliss lit up a cigarette. Smoking was still frowned upon by my mama's friends, but S. Bliss did as she pleased and she seemed to please most folks most of the time.

"Did you two hear me? I said you lovely creatures are surely the belles of this ball."

"You think so honestly, Mama?" Liliane queried, taking on all her mother's smooth motions and impenetrable demeanor, knowing the answer could only be yes.

I was still fiddling with my hair. The french roll I wanted was tumbling instead of fixing. S. Bliss walked over to me, put some hairpins in her mouth, commenced to setting my "look" right.

"Do you think the conference was a success, Mrs. Lincoln?" That's what I asked her, cause I knew she had no time for dim-witted girls.

"That depends on what you mean by success, Roxie. Is the Negro going to be really free at say midnight tonight, no. Are we going to be free of the insanity of Jim Crow by dawn, absolutely not. But you girls have to realize the freedom you wage your most serious battle for is your very own mind. No white man on this earth has the power or the right, for that matter, to control a single inch of your brain. Your minds, girls, are the first battlefields for freedom. You understand me." When she was talking, I kept thinking how odd this all was. Here was somebody's mother, Liliane's actually, with hairpins in her mouth, tending to another child's grooming, going on about our minds. Then my mama, R.C., stepped through my door glistening with excitement.

"Oh, S. Bliss, we got that Ruth Brown record we were looking for. Girls, are you leaving this old woman out of your goin's-on? I'm mighty sprightly myself, you hear. We are going to do all those dances I told you about, Roxie. What you call old-fashioned, but you'll see, won't she, Bliss? There's a whole lot of sugar left in this here, R.C. Golightly. Yes, there is."

My mama took over from S. Bliss with my hair and my powder for my forehead and my nose where I usually shine. As was her custom, Mama muttered, "Young men don't want to see any shiny colored girls. They want to see their faces in your eyes, not riding on your nose."

Liliane, S. Bliss, Mama, and I were a-twitter. It was like they were girls again too. Then I heard Liliane's father, Parnell, shout up for S. Bliss. She excused herself. That's when I realized she could get nervous. She rushed so, leaving, that her dress got caught on the knob of my door. Then, instead of working the cloth off, she just ripped it. Ripped that gorgeous peach organza. I saw Liliane blush and start to brush her hair again. S. Bliss blushed and ran on down the stairs toward Mr. Lincoln's voice. I'd never seen a mother and a daughter blush, simultaneously, before. When I looked to my mama, she lowered her eyes. I wasn't about to lower my eyes, but I did keep my mouth shut.

By the time night fell, the cicadas were singing, the music

was just blaring, and Liliane and I had ventured to the back of the yard with some African students from Tougaloo, Granville Simeons from Nassau, and a punch Mama had had made up for us. "No Jack Daniel's for your fast little behinds," she'd chuckled. We were trying to learn the high-life from Abe-Odun, but the grown-ups kept switchin' the records. Liliane pulled me aside, whispering that she knew what was up.

"I bet our mamas are looking for that Ruth Brown record. My father thinks it's so lowdown. He doesn't like to hear it, but he sure 'nough doesn't mind looking at Ruth Brown." We picked through the bushes to get a look. There was R.C. and S. Bliss by the record player, all hands and 33 LPs. All of a sudden there she was, in all her honky-tonk glory:

*"I usedta drink, I usedta smoke, I usedta do the*
*hoochie-coochie*
*I usedta drink, I usedta smoke, I usedta do the*
*hoochie-coochie*
*And now I'm saved, I say I'm saved. Oh, I'm saved."*

S. Bliss was in a writhing flirt. R.C. a twirl in my father's arms. Even the white men, all two of them, were patting their feet to that big drum beat: boom, boom, boom. Abe-Odun, the Simeons, and Liliane and I were mastering the high-life neath the Spanish moss, when there was a boom bigger than the drum.

"Get down. Get down," I shouted. I knew, in spite of the sound of Ruth Brown's voice brazen in the air, I knew these boom sounds weren't to keep us dancing the high-life or the mess-around. This was the boom and crash and shriek of night-riders, of Ku Kluxers, of our tormentors.

"Get down, you fools, get down. Don't you see, it's the Klan."

We were lucky, you see, cause those cracker dogs didn't stop their cars and come kill us one by one. The front of the house was scorched, the porch all off and such, but nobody was hurt by bullets or fire. That's because crackers are so stupid, my papa said. After a bit of commotion and a rudimentary visit from the constable, who I thought must be related to Bull Conner, things quieted. Of course, the constable suggested we send everybody home for their own good, you see. But it was S. Bliss who stood her ground.

"I appreciate your concern, officer, but I'm sure our friends aren't going to allow a small mishap to interfere with the festivities. As you can tell, not only the Negroes in Biloxi know how important the Defense Fund is, and we most certainly will not be allowing white trash in used cars to determine when we go home."

That's what she said. I must say, my mouth fell open. I looked for my mama, who could talk sense, but she was right beside S. Bliss, holding her arm actually. Parnell Lincoln and my papa, Mathias Golightly, were right behind them, too.

Lincoln Parnell stepped over to the constable, who looked so red and wet he must have smelled like a beat dog. Anyway, Lincoln Parnell asked the constable if that was all. He turned his flat nasty white behind around, and started to walk out. I could hear him saying: "Some Nigras just don't know what's good for em."

Then I saw my papa with a passel of shotguns. He handed

them out to whoever would take one. Not everybody did. Papa and Parnell Lincoln went to take watch out front. But before they went, I could hear them laughing menfolk-laughing, that's slow and couched in cussing: "Put Ruth Brown back on that machine. To hell with these white folks."

> *"I usedta drink, I usedta cuss, I usedta do the*
> *hoochie-coochie*
> *I usedta drink, I usedta fight, I usedta do the*
> *hoochie-coochie*
> *I usedta fight . . . I usedta fight,*
> *I usedta fight . . ."*

Yes, Fidel, I thought. We're dancing and fighting in Biloxi. This is Biloxi's mambo. I'm going to wish it all the way to Havana. Me and Ruth Brown.

# Room in the Dark

# III

——— Deconstructionists will say it doesn't matter. The word, per se, no matter where we put it, is lacking. . . . Deconstructionists'll sell they mama for a proper signifier or a sign.

———

——— Oh shit. Before I can get to what I really wanta talk about I've gotta deal with this "qualifiers" idea. The, what you call, the quality of the sign—the signal . . .

———

——— The signifier may be related to a gesture I cannot misinterpret, which is why I like this guy. . . .

———

——— I, this man, I mean, Jesus, nobody'd understand.

——— Why not?

——— This guy I been associatin' with . . . huh . . .

——— Yes.
——— Well, we just dance. We dance all the time.
———
——— Yes. We go out sometimes. I get all dressed up and we go dancin'.
———
——— Something frilly with big loopin' earrings I wear, but you don't know. Sometimes I put on really sexy clothes, chiffon skirts and things so tight nobody believes I could take them off, not even in the shower. He dances with me.
———
——— Then, after he dances with me, he makes such a great omelet with cheddar cheese and some small enticing avocados. He wants to bomba.
——— But you say this guy likes to dance.
——— It's 10:30 A.M. in the mornin'. We've no clothes on. Why would we? It's the mornin'.
———
——— Actually, I'm not tellin' you everythin'.
———
——— It's not that I'm lyin', I just forgot to tell you about these . . . contests we usedta win.
——— Contests?
——— Yeah. We were so poor. Well, not white people's poor. We usedta win these salsa dance contests at this place on Valencia in the Mission that had just discovered that everybody wasn't from Jalisco. No. I shouldn't say that. It's not fair.

———

——— But there was no way they were gonna take that twenty-five dollars from the two of us.

——— Isn't this a new person?

——— Yes.

———

——— Why?

——— You're saying "us" and "we" so easily, that's all.

——— Well, if you did get a chance to dance with him, you wouldn't want to be one of them either. Definitely one of us, that's how my daddy would say it. "One of us."

——— He's a good dancer?

——— Who? Daddy? Oh my God, yes! Oh, you are being so smart. My daddy dances with my mother. The contests they won were on these boats that the city of Akron could fit in where they never forgot they were colored, but it didn't hurt so much.

——— Where was that?

——— At sea, Jesus, sometimes you are very slow.

———

——— Suave. Suave. Slow. That means slow and smooth, soft. His hands are very soft, almost like damp silk, you know, and we've no clothes on. So we just ate breakfast in bed. I could have stayed asleep. I sleep so well there, with him. Like I'm so relaxed, so much at home I could have stayed home, I sleep through too much of my visits with him. I don't want to, but I lose track of my bones, the skeleton, ha, and melt into this mound of flesh, warm. I feel so warm there. Do you think when I'm sleeping like that I feel like damp silk, too?

——— Undoubtedly.

——— Don't make fun of me.

——— Why do you think I would make fun of you? This all sounds rather delightful to me.

——— Really?

——— Yes.

———

———

——— I really could just stay asleep there . . . til he comes sayin', "Darling, it's time to eat now." What could I do?

——— Sounds like you could do anything you want with this fellow.

——— I mean, I'm so sleeping away and sighing, but I've gotta eat, right now, cause cold breakfasts are truly terrible, don't you think? I wanta tell him how good it all is. The eggs aren't runny or too brown. I can't tolerate brown, burned eggs. I can't stand the smell of them. So these eggs that he'd made were bright yellow and fluffy, like cotton candy they were. They weren't lukewarm either. Oh, he put such seasonings.

———

——— Do you believe there are men who aren't bein' paid who go to such trouble?

———

——— Well. Hey, I usedta didn't, but now I do.

———

——— Oh God, he's funny. He stands up, just so fulla himself. Got a real cute butt, now that I think of it. A backside that sorta flirts with me in spite of myself. . . . So there is my mambo man with his flirtatious behind straightening his shirt in front of the windows. This boy don't have no shirt on. He's quite amiably wonderfully naked. Jesus . . .

———

——— Whatta fool, hum. Well, once his shirt is all tucked in and his creases in his pants straightened. He might as well have put on a tie and a top hat roamin' round butt-naked like that, naked as a jay bird, but with élan, you know. So he starts to push these chairs out of his mambo path with a ferocity, ah, a man obsessed, and says in one of those voices I imagined when I was little, he says and it's like a stream of wet gold floats by my face his words are like that, "Would you like to mambo with me?"

———

——— These things don't happen to people. Things as lovely as this don't happen to people like me at least.

———

——— I must sound ridiculous.

——— What does it matter?

——— I don't know. It's just I'm grinning about something you don't know and I don't believe it happens, that's all. Cause I said "Yes." "Yes, I wanna mambo with you." I said "Yes." How could I say no?

———

——— How could anybody say no?

——— Why would you say no to a guy standin' in a window, naked, as you say, who just wants to dance?

——— On the other side of that window, sir, is the one and only Paradise Cafe.

———

——— It's this bristling lime and yellow bar with a sometimey neon sign over the door. Pa adis  Caf . That's so funny, something missing from paradise.

———

——— I almost feel like I'm in Laredo or Tijuana, but we're not. He's never spent no time near the border or places like El Paso and Matamoras. Oh, the bars are just as tiny and carnal, carnal. . . .

———

——— But he's not part of that landscape. . . . We're somewhere in flashing lights, green, red, gold, blue, like Christmas all the time. And we are the ones who can hear *"Amame y besame, amor. Besame, amor, besame."* The light is so precious that the notion of high noon in South Texas is an affront to our senses. And off we go to bomba on a new floor. To mambo like a baptism or an oblation. Two swayin' bronze bodies teasin' the mornin' sun that licks at us . . . our smiles curve cross our lips, maybe our smiles even curve across our hips.

———

——— Are you listenin' to me?

——— Yes, of course.

——— You know what I like best?

——— No.

——— I like the way the white lace handkerchief is in his hand. He's holdin' his hand up in the air like this. See? This dash of white is just above his shoulder and draws my eyes to his. So I'm not even in my own body.

———

———

——— Where are you?

——— Our tongues fly like tropical flowers in a *ciclón.* I'ma treasure I can't afford. I cannot even keep. That's why I'm in his eyes, his eyes, or the air, very hot humid air. Somehow he manages to have me turn under myself. Like this, watch my arm. Yes, like that, but more delicately. And when I'm in perfect rhythm, I am his body and mine, moving through each other. Our nipples are the accents of some rhythm Mongo Santamaria or Pablo "Potato" Valdez would find irresistible. He says to me only, "Shimmy."

———

——— I do. . . .

———

——— I . . . do. I do and I blush. And I do dance with him.

———

——— But we just finished breakfast. It's broad daylight. People are eating Sabrett's frankfurters and bagels. Katz's is open.

———

——— Well, can't you see?

——— What am I missing?

——— They can't really talk to me without signifiers or signs.

———

——— They can't talk to me without preconditions, assured levels of literacy.

——— Yes.

——— Well, what I'm saying, what I mean to say is that he feeds me. Then, we dance.

———

——— He gives me fluffed rice, mangoes, and fried chicken. And we dance.

———

——— He ties my shoelaces and unties my bustier with his teeth. Did you know I hadda bustier?

——— No.

——— It's black and rose lace with stays.

———

——— All I know is he feeds me and we dance. Why he even gives me tokens and we go somewhere else and dance. Sometimes we get transfers and find more places to mambo.

———

——— Now he's helpin' me perfect spins. Perfect spins. See, watch me.

———

———

——— That's like mastering the "turn" of a phrase, don't you think? So, I repeat, what's missing in Paradise?

——— Well, I had this dream. Do we have time?

——— We've about seven minutes.

——— Okay. My friend Michelle and I are on our way from my house, the one in the Fifth Ward. We go down a tiny alley that doesn't really exist to see someone I don't know. Another black woman who has two children and a shop. She lives upstairs. The shop is draped with textiles, sculpture with the usual Navajo and West African motifs as well as straw, dirt, and stone pieces. There are some glowing arclike things in the shapes of headdresses from the Moulin Rouge which I really want. There's no price tag. There are other things, wall hangings of red, brown, and black mud-cloth that I think would do well as ponchos, but the woman says the cloth cannot be cut. Later we go toward a river where there's a restaurant I've never seen before. It's all decked out for St. Patrick's Day in green streamers and shamrocks. It is very elegant, very grand. On a spiral staircase there are green-clad chorus girls doin' battements and carrying trays of champagne-filled glasses. At the bottom of the stairs there is a small group of girls, two black and one white, doing a sand-dance. They are wearin' kilts and tams. I notice the black ones' faces are painted and each one has different braids patterned on her head. I wonder how their mother managed to get them to rehearsal on time. Michelle says she knows who they must have studied with, but don't know how to get to that studio. I am hungry. We've no reservations and the place is packed with white people in formal garb and blackface. I search for an exit. I'm so disappointed, but I panic because the blackfaced crowd is becoming unruly and I cannot find the door. I can't find my way home.

———

——— Do you understand me?

——— What do you think, I don't dance with you?

*''El Bochinche''* *es que*
*only* Fe Cortijo *Knows*
or
All the LeBron Brothers
Know If
Victor-Jésus María
Sang Lili to Her Freedom

And like Pete "El Conde" Rodriguez, smelling like warm cognac, pure and sweet sweat *que toca* the sidewalk like Pacheco, I saw her, *la gringa negra* and her body was singing to me. No, really. Listen. Listen to her stroll Avenue C. *"Canta, canta, canta mi cancion, querida. Canta, canta, mi querida, canta mi cancion."* I admit there's every possibility that Liliane, I always call her *"mi luchadora,"* she had no image of me before I took her, captured her, however you wanna say it in English. I'm in charge of *visiones del sur,* south of 6th Street and anything between 1st Avenue and the East River *esta mi corazón, esta mi tierra.* I'll fight for it and I'll love it, *mira,* I make it black and white, two-dimensional, *con claridad* once I get *una cosa* that no one else seems to be able to see; once I get *la cosita* in a photograph: There's no gettin' away. So I mambo with long legs. Challenge telephone poles, carnal. That's chicano talk. I'm telling you I whipped around *la gringa negra* like all of El Gran Combo on New Year's Eve. She startled, stepped back and ba-tum, I took her picture.

I smiled, relaxed, moved out of her way, but she was mine. *Tu m'en tiende, yo tengo su cara* and when she walks her limbs cry out like a *mulatta* who never tasted fresh coconut milk, at least not from Puerto Rico.

But that's a lie, just like the camera lies. When I catch what nobody wants anybody to know just wafting cross their cheeks, trickling out the side of their eyes, a shallowness or a hurt allegedly disguised. I lied about meeting Liliane, myself, the pace of it. I wished I coulda been alla that for her, *mi luchadora negra,* but like Felipe said years ago, "I'm nothin' but a Spanish-speaking colored kid." So what would Liliane want with me? I asked her once, but her English was not only syncopated, it was multisyllabic, but I ain't really no different than her in the gut. I could see things, even invisible things. Anyway, one time I said to her black ass, *negra,* what do you want with me? And she said something about a "man" and language. That was a bit much, you know. Just bopping over my head. So I 'plained. Listen, *querida, cajones* is the problem on the Lower East Side, the Loaisida.

First, take a quick look down any of those mean streets, baby, and you can line up the "able-bodied": able to shoot smack, able to fuck kids, able to make a home outta a tumblin' down assortment of rooms with no heat, no runnin' water, and a broken-down toilet. Look down the street, man, and see the fiercesome beauty of the young girls' bows, their mother's fingernails, and immaculate kitchens. Watch the lost Ricans find themselves homes, building after building, brick by brick, learning plumbin' and electricity like that, see the junkies rip it out later on tonight like tearing their grandma's, *sus abuela's,* hearts right out. Raunchy *corazón,* is what I call it. The hip boys wishing for more evidence of their masculinity lie up by our window blarin' the latest *merengue* from Santa Domingo. Askin' em to quiet down is takin' yourself for an Anglo, some fool imaginin' he could put a halt to *la fuerza* of our presence. Can you get to that? Cause you can't play radios on the trains, white folks believe we done lost our music. Ain't that a gas? Like what they can't hear just don't exist, man. But at night the Caribbean oozes out of the streets, *negra,* like how I'm gonna do you, right? Tell me, I'm lyin', *querida,* can you tell me I'm lying, Liliane. C'mon.

We laughed and fucked some more. We don't seem to have no bilingual or multicultural dilemma gettin' to some primeval state of being. Actually, I always thought it was funny that this little bitch talkin' all the time using English vocabulary, this sassy-assed gal could hardly say hello in Spanish, but could talk her way all over Fort-de-France, she didn't do nothin' but scream when we did what it was we did. Now, this is East 6th Street and ain't a lot gone down anywhere that ain't gone down here but I always gave my baby, *mi luchadora,* a pillow she could bite on. Then I'd turn up Willie Colon's anything real loud. She liked Colon. Knew all the brass choruses, every trombone solo by heart. Between him and his mouthpiece and her body and my tongue, she was speakin' all kinds of languages. Sometimes, she'd admit that she saw the same things I saw in the faces of our people, but that took time and careful questioning to get her to say yes she saw what I saw, how I saw it and when I saw it. She'd swear to me that our visions were the same. But she was so hard-headed, I couldn't possibly take her word for it the first time she figured out how to say something to me that might make me stop. I mean to leave her talking whatever tongue those groans that creep from her thighs to her mouth might be speaking. Now I'm a nice fella but I had to get her to where she spoke my language; I had to get her to where she knew wasn't nobody could understand her but me. Nobody could insist that particular tongue but me. Ever. Not a soul.

Liliane insisted, as she had to; she was an intellectual. The girl truly believed certain thoughts, even certain gestures, were impossible in certain languages. She was driven, by some power I never understood, to learn every language, slave language, any black person in the Western Hemisphere ever spoke. She felt incomplete in English, a little better in Spanish, totally joyous in French, and pious in Portuguese. When she discovered Gullah and papiamento, she was beside herself. I kept tellin' her wasn't no protection from folks hatin' the way we looked in any slave owner's language, but she had to believe there was a way to talk herself outta five hundred years of disdain, five hundred years of dying cause there is no word in any one of those damn languages where we are simply alive and not enveloped by scorn, contempt, or pity. There's no word for us. I kept tellin' her. No words, but what we say to each other that nobody can interpret.

And when she'd get quiet and her legs sorta swayed by my shoulders like palm leaves, then, I'd start to sing to her thighs again, her navel, the sides of her pussy would glow, be soakin'. She'd speak my language to me again. I'd give her back the pillow and turn Cortigo up high. She'd make like she didn't understand a lot of what I'd say to her, but if she got on my nerves, I'd put on Ismael Quintano. *Mua.* She'd either start taking off her clothes or talkin' to me like she knew I had some goddamn sense. I hadda great sense of her, but that's not enough to keep her. Not the way I used to have her, regular, wild, relentless and soft as a tropical surf. My Liliane, she said she can't keep giving in like that. That's how she put it, being taken to some other tongue. She called it giving in. I called it being mine. She said that was ontologically impossible. Of course, I threw her the pillow again.

But she's gone. . . .

> *She-ee-ee's—go-oh-oh-oh-ne,*
> *My baaa-be lef' me,*
> *Be-lieeh-eh-eh-ve me,*
> *She's gone, gone, goooohne.*

Left me at her opening, I guess, *La Luta Continua* applied to me as well as to South Africa. Anyways, there was this story I toldt her one night after she was sighing—humming the way I could make her talk, that tongue, *mi lengua negra.* I toldt her this story I wanted to make a photographic novel, à la Duane Michaels, and I wanted her for it. Now, I know I want more than that, but some ideas don't bode well *con una mujer, come mi comba tiente morena, mi dulce negrita, mi negra mohada.*

The apartment wasn't much, wasn't nothin' really. There was the proverbial tub in the kitchen and a real live closet for a W.C. More overwhelming was the insecticide from the bodega downstairs. I kept tastin' plantains, yellow and green ones, cassava, yuca, all kindsa greens, apples, oranges, everything, tastin' like dead mice or barely crawlin' cucarachas. Everythin' for us to eat, poisoned long 'fore smack was runnin' through our veins, 'fore grass smoke rings swirled through the stairway, way 'fore coke had us all thinkin' we was the genius of Velazquez, Picasso, Rivera by a multiple of Einsteins. Just the small *y el ritmo* held my photographs round my baby, kept her protected from the elements, left her in my hands for my eyes.

That's why I'd always tell Señor Medina to pick me an avocado that *mujere,* Liliane, would pick up. He ran the bodega with his wife who was simply the make-believe eyebrow woman to me. She plucked out all her eyebrows and assiduously drew her new daring black ones on her face like every hour and a half. Her name was Soledad, but I just call her *"ojos."* She liked that, bet that crotch even tingled some thinkin' I was swayed by her looks. Anyway, I could just see Liliane, pissed as hell, askin' for this avocado that she knew I coulda gotten myself, but I convinced her I didn't ask her for much, not like a real Latina, I mean. And I knew the Medinas wouldn't speak English to her cause it was beyond their version of the world that *mi negra linda* wasn't a *morena* at all, but a regular niggah. And I could see Liliane embarrassed when the gringo blacks listened to her speak Spanish and subtly disown her. I figured she needed that every once in a while. *Y,* if she's not gonna give me any babies, the least she could do is bring me an avocado, *sí?*

Gotta keep her on her toes, ya know, a bit off balance, outta focus. It's not like we lived in some sorta black-and-white frame. Well, that'd be pretty difficult considering the way Liliane looked at things. She saw the most pristine forms, dazzling color in anythin'. She felt the texture of stuff: rice, skin, water, the ringlets of black naps on my chest. I couldn't have forced her vision to be any less, but I tried til it was no more use. We didn't really go out 'cept round the neighborhood. How many social clubs with little red lights, a ghetto box, a pool table, and Budweiser beer can you go to? How many Nuyorican poets can ya listen to shout about the righteousness of the FALN and a free Puerto Rico?

Once Liliane tried to get me to go to Casa de Nuestro Mundo for Borinquen extravaganza: poets and performance artists from the island and all us Nuyoricans. I told her I wasn't going cause I wasn't into being snubbed by white Latins from Ponce or San Juan whose legitimacy was founded on how well they spoke Spanish and how uncolored they were. Like most descendants of slaves from any place, Liliane was committed to the notion that slavery some other where in some other tongue was less pernicious than what she knew. I read Guillén to her, Luis Palos Matos, Pedro Albiza Campos, Jose Luis González. I read to her in Spanish all about the scum, the vicious degradation of our people by Spaniards, *criollos,* and their precious mulattos. But like a child who's gotta have her hands held in the fire to know it burns, off she went. And the Spanish-speakin' white boys went crazy, when the spanglesh-speakin', maybe only English-speakin', maybe not white enough mainland Ricans performed. She had to get out the way of flying chairs and fists cause the white boys, *los blancos,* felt their true heritage violated by the hybrid: by the colored hue of the language we created and our skins as telling and African as the *bata.* One more illusion lost. I just asked her why she thought I callt her *mi negra.* Why from me the word would never hurt: *negra, mi negra,* Liliane. Don't you understand bringin' one bloody colored Rican in the house, bathing him, nursing him, giving him money to get out of town is not gonna free Puerto Rico. Gettin' bullets taken outta the limbs of *independisto's* women, that ain't gonna free Puerto Rico. It ain't gonna free you neither, *negra, mi negra bella,* when they land on your bell in the middle of the night or an O.D. or with the hell beat out of em by some more radical *independistos* or *anti-independistos.* They was too out of it to know more than somethin' happened, man. Can you and Lili help me out? This once, man, okay? Liliane'd always go to some corner and begin some ritual or other with candles and fruit, pictures of the Virgin Mary, Santa Barbara, Santa Cecilia, San Raphael. She'd hum her rosary and look at me til I felt my bones ache from the hurt welling from her eyes, or her mouth. Her mouth hadda way of curlin' round itself, like when ya eatin' pomegranates I'd see her like that with her lips, makin' shapes like she was tryin' to drink me, all my juices, and I'd forget whoever was round and I'd have to have her talk, just for me, just the way our language is, and sometimes she'd curse me, push or throw one of her sacred objects, but she would talk and she would go get the cassette for me. Then her face was calm. Then I knew, she'd let go of everythin' but me. I'm smilin' now, cuz once the music was on, her eyes closed and I told her what she'd see and she answered me, in my tongue. Sometimes, she almost prayed in my tongue and then I'd tell her a story. I'd hold her and tell her, keep your eyes closed and listen. *Escuchame. Escuchame cariña.*

Liliane's favorite story, when she was dripping and naked, especially if she was tremblin' and holdin' me so she wouldn't leap off the bed, her favorite story was about a young girl at the Corso for the first time. This is how it goes. Once upon a time a young girl, a pretty young girl, *una morena,* bronze like you with the piquancy of a ginger flower, adorned herself in organdy and silk. She tugged at a very loud garter belt and slowly wound brand-new stockings up her long legs. She stuffed taffeta slip upon taffeta slip neath the swing of her skirts and giggled at herself in the mirror, dabbing rose lipstick from one end of her smile to the other. She put her lovely feet, toes wigglin' to dance, she put them toes in a pair of fancy cloth shoes with rhinestone butterflies twirlin' about her heels. Yes, she did. Then she tossed a velvet shawl round her shoulders and was off to the Corso.

The East Side train was not quite an appropriate carriage for such a *flaca tan linda,* but she rode the ske-dat-tlin' bobbin' train as if it were the *QE 2.* At 86th Street she ran into a mess of young brothahs who callt to her, whispered, whistled, circled her, ran up behind her, got close enough to smell her, made her change her direction once or twice, til they realized she was determined to walk up the steps to the Corso and they couldn't, cause they had rubber-soled shoes. We all knew you can't wear rubber-soled shoes on the glorious floor of the Corso. So, *cariña,* the young girl who looked so beautiful, she looked almost as lovely as you do now, *chica.* She sashayed by the bar, through the tables crowded with every kinda Latin ever heard of, and stationed herself immediately in front of *El Maraquero* in the aqua lamé suit. *Oigame, negreta.* His skin was smooth as a star-strewn *portegria* night, see, like me, *negra.* Put your hand right there by my chin. Now, his bones jut through this face with the grace of Arawak deities. Like that, see. Now, run your fingers through my mustache *porque* his lips blessed the universe with a hallowed, taunting voice; high, high *como* a cherub, yes, a Bronx boy on a rooftop serenading his *amante, sí.* The way I speak to you, now, *sí.* This young girl was mesmerized. She was how you say when you bein' *bourgesa,* "smitten," right? No, don't move your fingers from my lips, not yet. But the most remarkable feature of *el maraquero,* what did her in, as we say, had the young pussy justa twitchin', ha, was *el ritmo* of the maracas in his hands. Ba-ba-ba/baba . . . Ba-ba-ba/baba. Oh, she could barely stand the tingling sounds so exact every beat, like an unremitant, *mira,* an unremitant waterfall, Ba-ba-ba/baba . . . Ba-ba-ba/baba . . . Ba-ba-ba/baba. Oh, she started to dance all by herself. It was as if your folks said the Holy Ghost done got holdt to her. She was flyin' round them bambos, introducing steps the Yorubans had forgotten about. She conjured the elegance of the first *danzón* and mixed it with twenty-first-century Avenue D salsa. The girl was gone. No, *dulce,* don't move your fingers. Here, let me kiss them. One by one. Cause that's what happened to the beautiful mad dancin' girl and our *maraquero.* For she was so happy movin' to the music he was makin' and she imagined he meant for this joy to overwhelm her. She started to cry ever so slightly. Let me kiss the other one. No not that one, the littlest one. With all her soul she thought he was tossin' those maracas through the air for her. So naturally her tears fell on the beat. No, don't laugh. Listen. Listen. The tears fell from her cheeks slowly and left aqua lamé streaks on her cheeks. Really. Then once they hit the floor; it was like a bolt of lightning hit *El Maraquero,* who jumped into an improvisation whenever one of them tears let go of that girl's body. Soon it was she who was keepin' *el ritmo* and he was out there on some *maraquero's sueño* of a solo. Now you know, *El Maraquero* has to be disciplined. He's gotta control, oh, the intricacies of Iberian and West African polyrhythms as they now exist in salsa music, right? Okay, let me have the other hand. No, I want to lick the palm of your other hand or I can't finish the story. You want me to finish the story, don't you? Well, good. Now I'll have kissed all your fingers and your palms and the bend in your arm. So *El Maraquero* became agitated. He wanted to know where his sound had gone, and to be honest so did the rest of the orchestra. Well, he hadn't noticed our beautiful young girl in her slips and organdy, her shoes with twirlin' butterflies. He wasn't like me, huh, he didn't see the surrender in her dancin' to his music. So he was astonished when he went to play and no sound came from the maracas. Our young girl, Liliane, who was so much like you, saw what he felt and she knew as he did not know that you do not own the beauty you create. Right, hear me. You don't own the beauty. Oh, I wanta kiss one of those rose tits of yours. No, I'm not finished with the story. Yes, let me nearer. No, don't move your fingers. *El Maraquero* is fuming. The young girl who's been dancin' and crying all filled up with something she can't call by name 'cept to say that she likes it. She starts cryin' inconsolably cuz *El Maraquero* has lost his music and she doesn't know where it is 'cept that not owning beauty doesn't mean you lose it. Well, let's see that finger again. No, I want the next one. No don't rush me. The young girl runs toward him and he's really pissed. I mean, no, I'm not pissed, I'm lickin' you, *pendeja.* He doesn't understand that he'll be playing no more music, no nothin', til he accepts that this young girl in her frilly dress and *mariposa* slippers has got holdt to his music. She's so upset about him not tink-tink-tink-tinktinkin' for her. Out of *desesperación* she starts to sing to him and one by one the seeds that had been her tears that had been her legs and hips dancin' to his *ritmo* all returned to the maracas and *El Maraquero* never lost sight of her again. Turn over. From then on, *negrita,* he played for his life every *cancion, cada coro,* cause his *chabala* would dance and cry his *ritmo* for him and then give it all back with her tears, her tears from feelin' what she had no name for, had never felt before, and couldn't do without. Right, Liliane, isn't that how it is for you?

Oh, she'd jump up and call me every lowdown exploitative muthafuckah in the world. It was "*chingathis*" and "*chingathat.*" "I'll be damned if it ain't some sick-assed voyeuristic photographer thinks his art is nurtured by a woman's tears." "Suck it, niggah," she'd scream, or sometimes she said, "Suck it, spic," if she was really mad. Then she'd turn around, tryin' to dress herself in this state. Something was always on backward or she put on mismatched shoes, threw my hat on her head steada hers. She'd go stormin' out saying, "My art is not dependent on fuckin' you or hurtin' you. Niggah, my art ain't gotta damn thing to do with your Puerto Rican behind. Besides you can't take pictures, anyway. Go study with Adal Maldonado, you black muthafuckah."

That's when I could watch her go down the avenue, wet and smellin' exactly how I left her. Then I watched all the other muthafuckahs just feel how she walked, talkin' under her breath in that butchered Spanish she talks when she's mad at me. I watch them watchin' her, and I know if I strolled down the street within the next hour I might as well be who I said I was in the beginning: Pete "El Conde" Rodriguez *que toca la música.* Only the instrument I played is named Liliane.

Musta worked her too hard. She don't come round anymore. Well, not for a while. *Canta, mi cancion, cariña, canta, canta.* "Speak my tongue, *negra,* it's good for ya. Liliane, I know I was good to you. Good to you. Hasn't Victor-Jésus María always bathed you in kisses, *com besos lideres?* Didn't I, *negra,* didn't I. . . ."

# Room in the Dark IV

——— So what do you want to do today?

——— We do what we usually do. You say what's on your mind; we go from there.

——— I don't want to talk about anything. I want to go home. That's what I want to do.

——— Okay. Let's go home, then.

——— That's clever. That's very clever. You know and I know that we're not going anywhere. This is a room with shadow light, a couch, a large soft chair, and a closed window.

——— Yes, that's true.

——— Well, then all this talk about going home is crazy. We're stuck in this room.

———

——— I mean, I know I came here voluntarily. I wanted to

come cause I'm coming out of my body. This is really odd. Parts of me, my feelings are streaming out of my hands and my thighs. I sense when I am walking that my thoughts are dripping down my calves from behind my knees. I am leaving puddles of myself underneath me and I can't pick myself back up, put myself back together.

——— Is that why you want to go home?

——— No, I left my house to come over here. Oh, this is really crazy.

——— You brought your crazy selves, that were falling away from you here. Maybe, this is their home. The slipping parts of you may need to be somewhere puddles of feelings aren't out of place.

——— This is a fuckin' mess.

——— I don't mind.

——— I do. I do. I do.

——— Why all this vehemence about a little messiness. People are messy creatures.

——— I just want to get myself together.

——— Like a puzzle?

——— What?

——— What parts are missing that keep you from being "together"?

——— Missing. What's missing? I forgot to tell you I lost a baby. I got rid of a baby.

———

——— I don't know. There was no way around it. Huh, I'm not the mother type, you know. I think they should come talkin' and potty-trained, you know. I

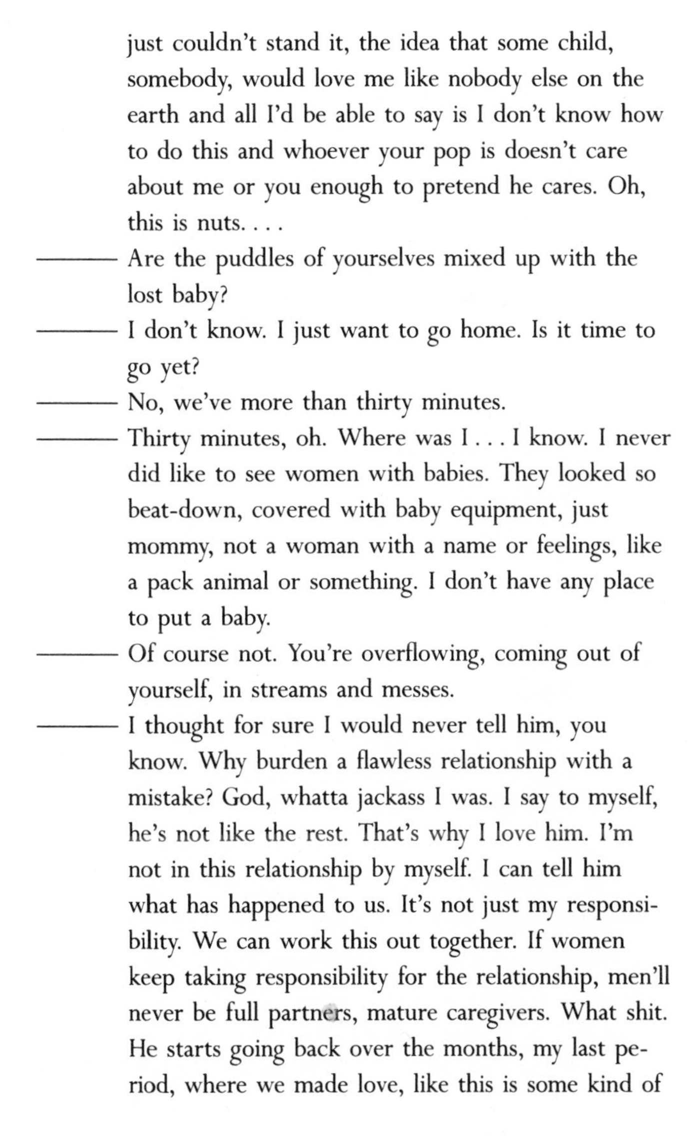

just couldn't stand it, the idea that some child, somebody, would love me like nobody else on the earth and all I'd be able to say is I don't know how to do this and whoever your pop is doesn't care about me or you enough to pretend he cares. Oh, this is nuts. . . .

——— Are the puddles of yourselves mixed up with the lost baby?

——— I don't know. I just want to go home. Is it time to go yet?

——— No, we've more than thirty minutes.

——— Thirty minutes, oh. Where was I . . . I know. I never did like to see women with babies. They looked so beat-down, covered with baby equipment, just mommy, not a woman with a name or feelings, like a pack animal or something. I don't have any place to put a baby.

——— Of course not. You're overflowing, coming out of yourself, in streams and messes.

——— I thought for sure I would never tell him, you know. Why burden a flawless relationship with a mistake? God, whatta jackass I was. I say to myself, he's not like the rest. That's why I love him. I'm not in this relationship by myself. I can tell him what has happened to us. It's not just my responsibility. We can work this out together. If women keep taking responsibility for the relationship, men'll never be full partners, mature caregivers. What shit. He starts going back over the months, my last period, where we made love, like this is some kind of scientific interrogation. My body is going to reveal to him how this happened. Like I'm a body of evidence. Jesus. We fucked. The sperm got out and found a egg. It's as simple as that. I know how we got pregnant. I want to know what we're going to do now. Not how did this happen. What kinda idiocy is that? Well, I covered my head with ostrich feathers and a red clay mask. Next thing I know I'm with child. Maybe we should call the news: "Woman inseminated by feather fetish." Or better yet, I think I'll hire a sky-writing plane and tell the world what I discovered: "Only the man you fuck doesn't know fuckin' makes you pregnant. Let's tell em." How's that?

——— Pretty expensive, those planes. Pretty dense feelings in those clouds where you're going to write the news.

——— I wanted to take the words back as soon as I said them. I wanted him not to know. He doesn't know. I couldn't stand him looking at me that way. I could not take it. How he looked at me.

——— What kind of look was it?

——— Like I had a disease or I was contaminated or stupid or clumsy.

——— You know you are none of those things.

——— I know. I know I can't stand to look at him, now. Not anymore. It's not like he didn't do his share. He drove me, waited, paid his half of the doctor's bill, brought me dinner. But it was so fuckin' obligatory like I was his sick relative or something heroic he'd done. He did.

———

——— Then, when I started bleeding, he got all hysterical. It wasn't much, just a little blood. I thought he was going to lose it. He says this is too much for him to take. He needs a break. I wished I'd had a gun, a brick, anything. It was too much for him. Was his body vacuumed, suctioned out of his groin like so much dirt? Did the nurse raise her eyes at him: too bad he doesn't love you all over her face. They took the check from my hand like there was blood on it. I looked to see if there was blood on my check, but it was on my leg. And he only saw a mess. Some complication my body presented to his emotional structures that used to cover me. They used to protect me, but now with the last remnants of this baby coating my legs, he's disgusted. Well, I'm glad. I'm glad I didn't have that baby cause if bloody messes are too much for him, then goddammit, he didn't love either one of us enough to be any itsy lil muthafuckin' part of our lives. He did not. He did not. Now . . . that's all.

——— That's quite a lot.

——— Yeah.

——— Now, we know why you think parts of yourself are falling out of you. You've got to pick up the baby and let her come into your life. You've got to own her, accept her.

——— I know. I want to do something for her birthday.
She's three years old tomorrow. I figured it out.
She's three tomorrow.

——— Liliane, it may be messy, but loving and grieving
don't cancel each other out.

——— I really want to go home now. I want to build a
house for her spirit to visit, somewhere close by me.
Make her a home.

——— Somewhere you can visit, too. Well, it's time.

# And Where Is Garnett Mimms?

There was something heretical about what was happening. Liliane, blushing and blurting, "What am I gonna do? What am I gonna do?" while five young men, all of whom had been her suitors, tried to preen and puff what was mussed, while the one cousin she was actually seeing kept kissing her. Later in life, Liliane would learn that that many young men who knew each other and you were probably a football team or a frat rush line engaged in a collegiate frivolity known as gang banging, then a misunderstanding, then she wanted it and finally date rape or wilding. If it took only one man to undo your dress and vertebral attachments during "rough sex" (a.k.a. rape), your hymen, labia, and vulva were considered more pristine and vulnerable than if you unfortunately had spent the night with some varsity team or other. Liliane wondered if the boys boasting about all the letters on their sweaters and pre-punk motorcycle jackets had ever thought of poor Hester Prynne. She had a letter too. A big red one. Probably sinny and silky, and did the cricket team have a yen for a girl with a scarlet *A*. Straight *A*s, as well as attentive, approachable, anxious to be somebody. Now that's an odd idea.

Anyway, this is not at all what was happening to Liliane the night her father arrived on Spring Street in Trenton to take her back to Bellmawr. Even then, everyone didn't go to the Bluffs or Bimini. Yes, Liliane's daddy poked the Mack truck of an El Dorado past the dignified row houses with porches and tended plants, past the women high in the last blush of their forties headin' for Klotz's, The Tuxedo Club. Some would even venture to The Candlelight or that one cross the wooden bridge over by Seward Street was just "the Bucket of Blood"—not a Bucket of Blood, but "the" Bucket. So here comes Liliane's daddy waving to everyone who might possibly see him on a stank dark Friday night looking like he was or hadta be the town's colored undertaker, colored tavern owner, colored dentist, colored lawyer, or colored doctor. Yeah, when Garnett Mimms was on every colored girl's mind and jolting every colored boy's body, the Negro's options were fairly limited. Liliane's options at that moment were particularly limited.

Liliane was a virgin. Liliane in a classical Catholic sense "belonged to no man" and was, therefore, bereft of sin. Liliane was a Daddy's girl.

And Daddy's girl was sprawled and hugged up, all at once mind you, sprawled and hugged up with Danny Stuyvesant, who was the more upwardly mobile among his cousins who had also courted Liliane since puberty. But this was getting to be almost grown-up and her panties were wet and her legs had thrown off her crinoline petticoat so that Danny Stuyvesant's leg could get between hers. Liliane's lips ached. She imagined she must be smiling too much, but that was impossible cause Danny's tongue was always somewhere in her mouth and his hands were everywhere, like hers, discovering all kinds of new rhythms. And Garnett Mimms sang on and Liliane's daddy strode on down Spring Street in the Twee-twee-tweedlie-dee of a Friday night, pausing here and there to chat and flirt. Some men feel women's looking at them a certain way demands at least a casual response: you know, sorta like noblesse oblige. Tickling little girls' necks while you talkin' up they mamas, blowing on a grown-lookin' sixteen's shoulder cause that's where your mouth happened to be leanin', smellin' on it the perfume of youth.

Liliane smelled herself and this was not dirt. This was more like she imagined first blood smelled if it had no color and capillaries fused from your lover's body to yours. This was the smell of fusion. Liliane exceled in physics, but was a dramatically pathetic biology student. Fusion, she knew. Biology, well, Danny's hands were explaining hers to her, how no one had ever even so much as touched. And cause it was dark in the cousin's aunt's bedroom, still no one had seen.

Liliane's head swirled. Her hips cried with every wail of Garnett Mimms on automatic downstairs where the rest writhed on two feet. Here in the dark with the one boy she'd gotten past Papa, Liliane saw the flowers from the hushed, just-bout-made-it wallpaper wandering her body like Danny's hands or thighs. When his mouth pounded on that muscle in her throat where every general practitioner in the world swore was a goiter, Liliane thought Danny was sucking her up the way the canal by Bellevue Avenue sucked up little ashy black boys in a flood. Liliane was floating. She was fallin'. Her dress was gettin' in the way of her tongue's trips cross Danny's cherry bronze cheeks. And Daddy kept movin' up Spring Street, ever so genteel.

There was still an earnest snobbery about doings on Spring Street. There were so many who lived two, three blocks east or west who'd have to wait another generation before they could say, "Well, you know, my daughter stays over there, you know, by Spring Street." Now, even though Liliane's papa, as she was wont to say sometime, was the only criminal court judge, colored, in the state, didn't nobody want to live out there where she did: 'mong a bunch of crackers thought Princeton was Mecca, reformed Jews who celebrated Easter, and them real colored over to "The Crossing." Now The Crossing had a name, but nobody used it. Wasn't no need. All you have to do is go straight on out Princeton Avenue, past Five Points, can't miss that. Big ol' pillar with George Washington standing a top of it and a pile of colored men dealin', talkin', drinkin', gamin', and eatin' fresh fried porgies from the shrimp boat cross the way. Well, go on by that and you'll see some projects. Now there's Negroes in there and a street callt Calhoun, but it had nothing to do with Calhoun the lawyer, who was a friend of Amos and Andy's. Well, past the projects you hit Rigidity Village. I mean, little prefab rowhouses puttin theyselves forward like make-believe white folks who worked in factories didn't live there. Everybody knew better than that. There's no signs for homemade kielbasa in Kingston, New Jersey. Anyway, all these make-believe white folks' names ended with vowels and quite often were assembled from a dumbfounding sequence of consonants, like Bryzinski, Scalia, etc. Once you got past this little feat of desperation, you'll hit Harney's Corner. It'll say that. Bear to your left and when you hit a sign that says there's traffic coming out from your left, but not from your right, then you turn left and you're at The Crossing. You'll know that cause no matter how often you drive down this little old unself-conscious street, you won't see any more Negroes, unless you run across Liliane and them. All the rest the way out there, past the Lawrenceville Prep School, the Toddy Shop and Bentley's Market, the Lawrenceville Presbyterian Church and cemetery, there's real white people with pedigrees from wars and ships, and Episcopalian Bible Date of Birth entries. Anyway, nobody wanted to live out there by The Crossing, though there was two bars that was a hoppin' and a boppin' over that way. Oh and if ya had decided to bear right at Harney's Corner, you'd have missed The Crossing, but you'd have gone by a house that freed Negroes have owned with their own land too, since before the War. Around here when they say "before the War," you really gotta catch yourself, cause they are referring to the Revolutionary War and not hardly all the colored or the make-believe white folks had set foot on this side of the earth yet. So, be vigilant in your dealings with these folks. Especially if you are Negro and don't know the differences tween the real white people and the make-believe ones. See, they may be imaginin' that cause they speak English as best they can, that they are real white people. That doesn't even hold water. But, lemme tell ya, brass knuckles, swingin' chains, zip guns, and tire irons done swayed many an arrogant young Negro's head about who be white and how and when he be it and if he be it good. Now, that's enough of that.

But this is where Liliane crafted a delicate social structure, penetrable only by her, and contrived for her desires and her protection. It was akin to Impressionism, Liliane believed. See, you pick up what gleams and stands out lovely from hardness and hushing up. You pull these startling elements onto a canvas of your own, and that's your life.

And Danny Stuyvesant was changing Liliane's universe. Daddy's presence had meandered solemnly and with a certain I-know-something-he-don't-know from one porch to another, til somebody who knew one of the cousins who knew which cousin Liliane was losing her mind with could tell somebody to go past the mass of grindin', wanderin' hands, sepia adagios, to get Liliane outta whatever she was in and wherever that was so she could look at herself before the Judge sauntered up the steps, tapping his foot, enjoying the niggahness of the music, and the much more significant appearance of his daughter, looking how she should, almost sculptured, sensually supple and innocent.

Liliane thought it was marauders pullin' at her, pullin' her way from Danny Stuyvesant's fascinating biceps. This is biology. "Oh, no. Not now," this is Liliane screaming and kicking at Danny's cousins, Matthew and Luke. Then, even Johnnie Boy came to help her help herself get together cause Papa was only two doors down the street. Liliane shot up straight like she knew something about male ritual. All she knew was her daddy was a hop, step, and a jump away. And all these young men who'd had no sisters—so they had never dressed a girl—they were hopping round Liliane, pullin' and tuggin'. Matthew dried her face with his handkerchief. Johnnie Boy was fixin' her slip. Luke was straightenin' out her bra and Danny Stuvyesant with no sense kept puttin' his tongue in her ear and runnin' his hands thru her hair till Johnnie Boy asked him how eager was he to go to Annondale Reformatory. "Remember, fool, her father's the Judge."

"Cry, Cry, Baby, Cry Baby" was all Liliane could hear. She didn't hear Danny saying he was coming out to the shore on Tuesday. She didn't hear herself giggle, sayin' what a good time she'd had and thankin' all the cousins for invitin' her; she didn't hear herself kiss her papa on his cheek and ask if he'd had a hard day. She heard her heart breakin' and some new place in her wishin' nobody had ever come in that room of flowers and Friday night temptation, wishin' there'd be no dawn, wishin' Danny had left the stars all up and down her thighs.

Judge Lincoln Parnell liked the drive thru Mercer County out Route 33 toward Freehold, the Circle, easing on to Asbury Park and finally Bellmawr Beach. As a boy, he'd "whupped" all those farm boys and factory workers' sons in any sport they could think up. Plus, now, he also sat in judgment on them, their ways, their snide superiority and dreams. Why, he'd been accepted at Yale with a full football scholarship until they saw him on the first day of practice. No colored quarterback. Impossible.

Princeton was the same, but meaner. They wondered did Lincoln Parnell realize that Robeson had gone to Rutgers, the state school. Now, had Lincoln Parnell ever lost a game or a woman? Didn't Lincoln Parnell graduate from everything before his older brothers had figured out they had to finish something?

Hadn't Lincoln Parnell's own pa tied him to a tree with a harness cause he wouldn't mind?

But Lincoln Parnell minded a lot of things. He minded the word "niggah." He minded the Scottsboro Boys, Emmett Till, Sam Cooke, and them constantly chasin' Chuck Berry. He minded Robeson's persecution; he minded we didn't own land, couldn't vote, could hardly talk and killed each other off whenever the white folks let up for a second. Lincoln Parnell minded and he kept score.

Liliane was counting, too. He kissed me 439 times, at least. He licked my eyebrows had to be five times. He pulled my dress down, oh, well, three times. He unbuttoned—let me see, how many buttons do I have—and she counted.

"Liliane."

"Yes, Papa."

"Looked like you all were having what we used to call a helluva good time."

"Sure did, Daddy. Why, I danced every dance and even did ole Ruthie whatshername, ya know the one who's dad is always up for disturbing the peace, well, I even did that little tramp out of the dance contest. I won, Daddy. Can you imagine, Papa? I won outta all the other girls there."

"No, Liliane. I'm not surprised. Sweetheart, you were always so light on your feet and could follow turns to any rhythm our people concocted from wherever. No, that's just my little girl. Too hot to handle, too smart to let go."

"Daddy."

"Yes?"

"Is this near where you and Mama drove into the cornfields

when you were young and before . . . you know, before I came?"

"Uh-uh. No. Was Route One-thirty, not Thirty-three."

"Oh."

Liliane was beginning to think that the clouds sinking toward the road were Danny's arms searchin' for her. She let the window down, so she could smell him. Her cloud-man.

She smiled, thanking the wind for bringing him so close to her, and the night was black and Judge Parnell loved to speed. Liliane started singing some, probably the Shirelles. Oh, it had to be "Will You Still Love Me Tomorrow." Judge Parnell watched his child, his little girl, making it with the wind and fog, singin' and grinnin'. A grin he'd seen many times before on the faces of young girls in love with young hoodlums he sent away from them. They never really believed til too late that their heartthrob, the being and reason for taking time to breathe, could just be outta reach for real, arbitrarily, or forever.

"You know, darlin', nothin's ever going to come of those boys in town there, where you were, I mean."

Liliane's jaws tightened. She refused to sit up quite straight, but she knew she couldn't make love to the wind.

"Well, Papa, you brought yourself up outta much worse."

"That's exactly what I mean, Liliane. Those boys have no fight in them, and with no fight a Negro man has no chance."

"That's ridiculous, Daddy. Why, you know every fella in there belonged to one of them gangs from the East Ward or the South Ward. Even the ones from The Crossing got a name of their own."

Judge Parnell sighed. He looked absently out the window. How was he gonna say what he said.

"Liliane, those fellas only got sense enough to fight for what little they know about. They don't have the backbone to fight for what's never happened, or for dreams."

"And what's dreaming gotta do with being called a niggah whore, or not being able to go to the Chapin School."

"Dreaming's got a whole goddamn sight to do with it. Look at DuBois, or even Dr. King, Nkrumah, or Charlie Parker. Those are men who never happened before and the world hasn't been the same since."

"Oh, Daddy, you already told me a courageous colored man is one with death on his heels."

"Right."

"What d'ya mean, 'right'?"

"Well, a man like that needs the kinda woman you're gonna be one of these days, if ya don't spoil yourself."

"Spoil myself?"

"That's what I said."

"Okay. Okay. So where are they? These rich little colored boys?"

"At the Bluffs, Kentucky Lakes, Rehoboth Beach, and McLean, Virginia."

"So why're you taking me to Bellmawr, then?"

"Oh, Liliane, you're still Daddy's secret."

*Cry Baby, Cry Baby, Cry Baby*
*Welcome back home*

—GARNETT MIMMS

# Room in the Dark V

——— So what do you want to do today?

——— What do you want to do? We can do anything you like.

——— I should have known you'd say that. "We can do whatever you want." Don't you ever get tired of being caught up in a bunch of neurotics' fantasies?

——— Is that what you think I do?

——— Well, how would I know actually? I mean, I can only extrapolate generalities from my experience with you. You know, move from the specific to the general, the universal where we are as one with each other in our ability to defy wisdom and keep doing the same ridiculous things that make us come here. . . . Come here to get particularly out of our universal sufferings.

——— Are you suffering today?

——— Not significantly. I'd say not to any great extent. I'm pullin' my own heart strings, I guess you can say that. I'm tuggin' my own heart strings. "Broken-hearted melody. Sing a song of love. . . ."

——— The last words are "Sing a song of love to me."

——— Oh really, is that what you'd like me to do, huh? Sing to you, croon a lyric of romance and passion?

——— If that's what you'd like to do.

——— But I can't do that. You're my analyst. How would it look for me to seduce my analyst. Then I'd be a real sickie, a raging nymphomaniac for real. I really need to do that. Get worse, so I can get better.

——— What might seem like, feel like, getting worse, whatever that is, may actually be a sign of getting better.

——— Right.

——— No, I mean it. The more easily you move through feelings or memories that you find terribly disturbing, the less dangerous these feelings are to you, the less likely you are to . . .

——— Awright. I feel like sucking your toes.

——— Hum. I don't think anyone has ever wanted to do that before.

——— Oh, come on. You're sort of cute, sometimes. I mean, some woman sometime must have wanted to suck your toes. You can't be that deprived.

——— What do you think?

——— What do you mean? "What do you think?" I told you what I think. It's impossible that somebody, man or woman, I don't mean to be presumptuous about your preference, but I know somebody must have sucked your toes, somebody must've.

———

——— Well, aren't you going to defend yourself?

——— I didn't know I was under attack.

——— Jesus, here I am offering my highly refined sensual skills and you think you're under attack. God, men are weird.

——— I didn't reject your lovely proposition in any way, Liliane. You introduced the sparring here.

——— Well, I don't want to talk about this anyway.

——— Okay.

——— Well, don't you see this is dangerous? What I said to you is dangerous.

——— No. How is that?

——— You know, sometimes, I think, you should pay me money. Shrinks and analysts, therapists, counselors, all you guys, can't let your patients, your clients, get personally involved. It's unethical.

——— Yes, unethical as well as criminal.

——— But who'd believe a woman who was seeing a shrink in the first place who said her shrink attack—seduced her. That's nuts in the get-go.

——— No, what's nuts is the professional who'd violate

those boundaries, take advantage of a trust, that vulnerability essential for treatment.

——— But they do it.

———

——— I know some who do it. Sleep with their clients. That's why I know I'm crazy. I gotta be crazy.

——— There's nothing crazy in what you just said. Nothing at all.

——— Well, say I had a lover who was a "counselor," I'm not going to say what kind, but say I was his lover and he confided in me that he had slept with his female patients, a few of them, sort of like he was doing them a favor. They were in great need, pain, some of them. So he fucked them.

——— How does that make you crazy?

——— Cause I was his lover. How could I be attracted to a man who had so little respect for another woman's confusion, her trust in him. He was supposed to help them, not fuck them. How did a dick get to be a cure for emotional problems. . . . No, wait. Freud's all up in here, shit. I didn't report him. You know, anonymously or anything. I didn't even stop seeing him for a while.

——— Is that why you are afraid now?

——— What the hell makes you say that?

——— Your legs are tucked up under you, your arms are clasped over your hips like you are protecting yourself from something, someone.

——— There's nothing going to hurt me in here. There's nobody else in this damn room but me and you.

——— Is that what's frightening?
——— What?
——— That only you and I are here?
——— What could you do to me? You just sit in that chair and suspend silences when you don't ask stupid questions. "What are you going to do to me?" Ha. You wish you could do something.
——— I am not going to seduce or attack you. I am not going to jeopardize myself and you in any way. Do you understand, Liliane?
——— Yeah.
———
——— Well, aren't you going to ask me do I understand, again?
——— No, I am virtually certain you believe I will not make any kind of overture.
——— Oh yeah, how do you know? I didn't say a thing.
——— No, but you're whippin' your legs in the air in a very sensual manner, and you're fondling your breast, to the right.
——— So what does that mean?
——— What do you think?
——— I guess it means . . . I guess it means if I want to say I feel like sucking your toes, I can go and feel like that.
——— And we can talk about it.
——— Talk about how it feels to suck your toes.
——— And how you imagine that makes me feel.
——— Jesus. Don't you ever give up?
——— Nope, but it's time.

——— Thank God.

———

——— I need to get out of here before I want to take your shirt off.

——— See you next week, Liliane. We'll talk about that.

——— "Betcha by golly, wow." *Ciao.*

# I Know Where Kansas City Is, But Did Wilbert Harrison Ever Get There?

Five generations of Malveaux had graduated St. Augustine's in New Orleans. Five generations of Malveaux had set the pace for the best of the race througout Louisiana. Why, through some parts of East Texas and western Mississippi folks would recount, with great seriousness, the accomplishments and achievements of this Creole phenomenon, the Malveaux, who could have turned their backs on their darker brothers, but did not, never had, and sposed ta never woulda, but Sawyer Malveaux III musta come from some extraordinarily recessive DNA combine. St. Emma's, the by-the-rules-for-you-rich-colored-boys-what-act-the-fool school, didn't even want him. This was not true for any girl named Emma, Raelene, Raelette, Nancy, Eugenia, Alexandria, Beth, Ann, Annie, Annabelle, or Liliane. That's me.

St. Louis in the spring break was a giant ball for young well-to-do Midwestern and Southeastern children of the Talented Tenth. Every other child I met was going to see me at Wellesley or Fisk. The young boys won cross-country and tennis scholarships to Yale and Princeton or Tennessee A&T. It depended on how one's parents felt about uplifting the race. Some would die before you went to Harvard. Some would die if you didn't. But that wasn't really the point. The issue was this issue: that we should crossbreed or intrafertilize and become the Beyond Belief Brood (offspring) of the Talented Tenth.

I knew I was part of this process. I'd yearned for what Papa had promised: a courageous colored man with enough niggah in him to make any niggah at ease and enough class to make them wonder about theirs. And this Sawyer Malveaux III could do without so much as lifting his pinkie, which he would sometimes do to make sure we knew his nails were manicured regularly. They were.

They were long, delicate fingers that arched and contracted. There was a spiderlike quality to his movements: practiced, intricate, manipulative, and beautiful. He liked that he was actually prettier than most of us; the one he chose, the one he let know he had decided against, and the poor creatures he didn't even see. He always walked into a party or strode the deck of someone's yacht as if Hannibal and his elephants in the Alps wasn't nothin', Foxes of Harrow and lil Inches's Mother he coulda written in his sleep one night and Jackie Wilson on the same stage as Chuck Jackson and Smokey Robinson singin' the Paragons and the Jester's greatest hits wasn't *nothin'*. Sawyer Malveaux III was an irredeemable hoodlum.

This rich colored boy who'd been thrown outta Morehouse, Tufts, Fisk, and finally St. Louis University, who'd wrecked a

TR 6, a hard-top Ford, and a vintage Jag, all replaced by Daddy. This faun in the thick and thin silk socks, who wiped his brow with silk handkerchiefs and would arrange for an abortion for anybody for $1,500, even had a process. No, I don't mean anything respectable-looking like Duke Ellington or Ray Robinson, but some wildass colored-looking "do" that challenged Brook Benton and Lil Richard. The boy had nerve.

It was his birthright.

I believed he was my destiny. We weren't like the others. I'd been raised round hoodlums, that's why I was farmed out on holidays: to see how the other half lived; broaden my horizons, you know. But truthfully, there was a ruffian in me that wasn't scared of him. Sawyer wasn't gonna be no failure or good-for-nothin'. He was what Daddy said. Someone we hadn't imagined and he knew it. He knew I knew it when he cruised by my cousin Lolly's porch and honked his horn. I was sposed to be beside myself and run-jump into the red Thunderbird and zoom . . . niggahs on Eastern Boulevard at twilight. Sure. So I called into the house, "Lolly, somebody out here needs directions, or is lost or something."

Lolly gave me the look of Maggie thinkin' of those no-necked children.

"Why, you know that's Sawyer Malveaux."

"Yes, I do."

"He's not here to see me. He's known me all my life."

"Umhummn, but if he's here to see me, he's gonna haveta talk. I don't understand car horn language."

And I sat there in the wrought-iron love seat staring at this incredibly brazen thing who was gonna have to come get me.

Of course he double-parked and left the radio blaring something by the Olympics. When I think about this, I make believe the Olympics were in the middle of Wabada Street in their lamé suits and those terrible-looking patent leather shoes justa jumpin' and posin' and singin', "Mine exclusively, mine exclusively," while Sawyer came up to ask me if I'd like to go for a ride.

I swear 'fore God my whole body was trembling with unmitigated delight.

"Why, Sawyer, surely you don't think I can just leave the front porch and go off on a ride with you. I'm not from here and you know how people talk."

"Awright, Liliane. It is Liliane, isn't it?"

"Umhummn."

"Where would you like to go?"

"I wanta go everywhere you like to go in East St. Louis . . . when you go by yourself."

"Oh, well. I'm not sure that . . ."

"But you asked me. It's not like you to refuse a lady, now is it, Mr. Malveaux."

He grabbed my hand and we almost ran—no, we did run down the lawn—to the curb. We were panting by the time we reached the car. When he opened my door for me, he asked, "They call you anything besides Liliane?" Stretching out the "aaannne."

"No, they do not."

"Well, today you're Lili, spelt just like that. Today, mind you, just for today, whenever I say, 'That's Lili, she's my new *girl,*' you smile."

"Every time?"

"Every time, or we sit here. You understand?"

"Umhummn, let's go."

So I am grinnin'—"Yes, that's Lili, she's my girl"—through all these games of pool. To help entertain myself, Sawyer showed me how to drink shots of tequila, lick salt off my hand or his, and chase it with some beer. He laughs at me. He thinks, Lili feelin' no pain is funny. Sawyer's fingers around the cue stick are so beautiful, I think I am goin' to start cryin'. He calls his sweet stick "Lili." I am gettin' confused. But before I can scream, "Do somethin' with me," Sawyer had spirited me to a room, a corner behind a floating crap game, some poker players, and a bevy of women with very long eyelashes.

I am still floatin'. Now I hover over the end of a long, long bar. I must be restin' in the palm of Sawyer's hands, where else is this possible? Sawyer talks dirty to me. He must be talkin' dirty to me cause my face is so red my body's caught fire. He laughs at me: his tongue sweeps the giggles from behind my lower lip. I gasp for air every time he shifts me in his palms. My mouth falls open if any one of his fingers caresses my temple.

I didn't want to laugh cause guys take sex so seriously, you know what I mean? But the top was down as we rode home; all the stars kissin' my face and neck and shoulders. The wind coaxed peculiar hummin' sounds from my mouth, while Sawyer's very beautiful fingers alternately strummed Bo Diddley licks. Chuck Jackson hollers from my pussy. I was in such a state. I've no idea how Sawyer got my panties off. No idea at all. I do know that he had them cause with his free hand, the one that wasn't playin' with my clit, he brushed them by his lips and mustache. "Good they're wet. I like that. I really like that, Lili." I knew I was goin' to faint, but I managed to sneak in the back of Aunt Aurelia's without stopping every time my pussy throbbed. It took me a long, long time to reach the door, though.

Somebody from East St. Louis shot Sawyer Malveaux III four times in the head a few years later. Everybody went to the funeral in Kansas City, even girls who'd been afraid to look him in the eye and their parents who prayed he'd straighten up and marry their girl, or just go to hell.

Sawyer was born into hell. Sawyer was the sixth generation of Creoles who decided not to turn their backs on their darker brothers. Sawyer was a brother. And Sawyer died.

While the other rich lil colored boys were hippies, Panthers, or in Canada, Sawyer died just like the little hoodlum boys I grew up with who lost all they sense or all they bones in Vietnam or Oakland. Sawyer wasn't all he coulda been, maybe. But like Papa used to say, he was definitely one of us. At the wake, his hair was done up like Sly Stone. The Malveaux family had his sister committed when she returned from Cornell one summer with a twelve-inch Creole Afro. She was never pretty. She didn't know Sawyer was a being more beautiful than she could hope. She didn't know Sawyer's rush was to be stunning. To stun any living thing. *Pauvre* Hyacinthe, delicate, mongrel-blooded, tragic mulatto didn't claim her birthright. She was a sixth-generation Malveaux. In our incestuous milieu the world was hers, but she let something or somebody define the territory. So, the lesson is Sawyer's dead and she's alive, if you can call tending Sawyer's mausoleum, all marble and pink granite, living. Hyacinthe (French pronunciation) lives on her trust and defiantly plants orchids in Missouri soil. There is no need for this. My drawings of Sawyer reveal such splendor, such irrepressible fervor to burst open, shower the planet with his scent. Hyacinthe never understood her name. But she does live in Kansas City, I guess. That's where Sawyer lives now, too.

*Goin' to Kansas City*
*Kansas City here I come*

*I'm going to Kansas City*
*Kansas City here I come*
*They got some crazy lil*
*Women there and I'm*
*Gonna get me one*

—WILBERT HARRISON

# Room in the Dark VI

——— I can't have therapy today.

——— That's the time we should work most intensely.

——— Listen, stop fuckin' around. I can't have no goddamned therapy this morning. I'm telling you. I don't think I can do anything today.

——— You already have done something. You came here.

——— He killed her. She's dead.

——— Who's dead?

——— My friend, Roxie. She's dead. He killed her this morning. Real early this mornin' . . . It was on the news. "Woman found strangled in bedroom, while child looked on." . . . I can't believe this. I just can't have therapy today, that's all.

——— I am very sorry to hear this, Liliane. I am.

———

——— Would you like to lie down or sit over in the chair by the window, perhaps.

——— No, I don't want to lie down. Dead people lie down. Roxie was in her bed lying down. That bastard. That cocksuckin' bastard.

——— You saw Roxie recently, didn't you, Lili?

——— Yes, of course. Our show opened two days ago. She had these wonderful jalapeño earrings on that lit up every ten seconds. The work was so strong too. Roxie was so happy, so happy, but I knew it. I knew she had to get away from that jackass. I knew it. And now, he's gone and killed her. Strangled her, stabbed her. I knew it. I knew it. Oh God. Oh, I knew. I could feel it.

——— But did Roxie know it?

——— Yes, we all told her. We told her over and over. This guy is not right, Roxie. Get him out of the house. We told her. . . . And Sierra saw this. This fool ties her mother's hands and feet with pantyhose, stabs her and chokes her. Oh God. Oh God. I feel like something's ripping me apart, tearing my soul up, tearin' me to pieces. . . . What can I do? Please, please, I don't know what to do.

——— Here's some tissue. . . . No need to rush or hurry, Liliane. Take time.

——— Time. Time. Take my time. I could've gone over there. I could have called to see if she was all right. I could have taken Sierra for the night. Oh, Jesus, what kind of friend am I? I knew something terrible was going to happen. I knew. I knew and I didn't do anything. I didn't do anything. Roxie's dead, murdered, and I didn't do anything.

——— Liliane. First. Hear me out now. First of all, you did not kill Roxie. I know this hurts. She meant a great deal to you. You loved her very much, but you did not kill Roxie or help her to get killed. You were her friend. She was not a friend to herself.

——— Shut up! Shut up! You don't understand. That muthafuckah was everywhere, all the time tellin' her that she was weak, she couldn't draw a straight line. She couldn't cook. She couldn't balance a checkbook. She dressed like a slut. She was a tramp with good luck. She was a pitiful mother. She didn't deserve the grants she got, the reviews. He said she didn't deserve him. Can you imagine. Him. And that bastard killed her.

——— That's right, Liliane. He killed her, not you.

——— But we told her. We tried to tell her. She called me at my workshop, you know, where I teach. She called me. She was so *frightened.* She had the secretaries track me down in the cafeteria. I jumped up and ran to a pay phone to get back to her and she was whispering that she wanted to see somebody quickly. She thought Sierra was in danger. She wanted to get out of the house, but I was at work. I said: "Come pick up my keys. You both can stay with me." She said that he'd think of us first. That that wasn't a good idea. I said: "Okay, come and get some money and go to a hotel." Then she had to go. She said: "I've got to go. I'll talk to you later.

Awright?" Like she wasn't scared anymore, like we were talking about a luncheon or something. I knew he must have come round. I knew in my bones, he must have come round.

———

——— Then, when I called her back that night, she said she was going out for dinner by the bridge with that dog, Tony. She swore she'd call me later. . . . When she called, she said they were going to get married. I couldn't believe it. Why are you going to marry a man who's jealous of your work, your friends, your child even? How could she marry somebody who made her so afraid, she'd just start cryin' sometimes for no reason at all. No reason at all. Just tremblin' so. I can see her now.

——— But did Roxie see anyone?

——— Well, she took your number. Then she said she didn't want to confide in a man.

——— Yes. I recall that.

——— And she did go a couple of times to that woman you recommended, but she stopped going because Tony said anything they needed to work out they could do together, she trusted him, didn't she? And she fell for it. She believed that fool. Jesus.

——— And not her friends like you.

——— It doesn't matter. It doesn't matter, now.

——— Yes, it does. It matters immensely. You loved Roxie very much, and Sierra. There's been a terrible tragedy that you will have to work through, realize you are not responsible for Roxie's death. Roxie is.

——— Fuck you! What in hell are you talkin' about? Roxie didn't strangle herself. She didn't put sixteen knife wounds up and down her body. She didn't tell Sierra: "Come, darlin', watch Tony kill Mommy."

——— Didn't she?

——— No. No! She didn't. She didn't. She did not.

——— Did she leave the house?

——— No.

——— Did she let Sierra stay with friends until she and Tony worked things out?

——— No. I told you, no.

——— Did she ask him to give her some time to herself, for her to work things out for herself?

——— No. She couldn't ask him something like that.

——— Did she discontinue her counseling?

——— Yes, but you don't understand. You don't understand. She was killed. He killed her. Said he heard God. Said the Lord was displeased with her painting and her friends. Her art and her friends were smut, the Devil's handiwork. That cocksucker no more heard God than I have a million dollars in the bank. The lyin' muthafuckah. Oh, my God. Roxie. Roxie. Why didn't you listen to me? Why didn't you listen to me?

———

——— He told her she couldn't do anything right. Nothing. He even told her she couldn't paint. Told her she couldn't paint. It was only cause she was a woman that she got so many breaks. Breaks, Roxie. Roxie. Why didn't you run away from him like the antelopes you carved could run. You know, Roxie had a piece from this last show. It's still hanging right now at the gallery. Her pieces are in the room next to mine. These antelopes are so delicate, two, three inches at the most, a fine misty gray flat stone she painted wildflowers all around them, glorious rose, yellows, and lavender flowers all around the antelopes. And over the antelopes, boughs of magnolia trees carved just as finely. Roxie used to say these were Southern antelopes, probably, resting near Lake Pontchatrain lapping murky brown swamp water of French roast and chicory. It's sold already. Somebody bought it, going to take it home, look at it, see the beauty of it, the odd humor and sweetness of it. Roxie, why didn't you listen to me. Why didn't you listen. . . .

——— Liliane, what's happening?

——— Sierra is crying that she wants to stay with Aunt Lili, cause I wasn't ready to leave the opening yet. We'd only been there bout an hour. People were still comin', but that jackass, Tony, pulled his junked-up car out front, wouldn't stop honking for Roxie to come outside. He refused to come see the show, said a bunch of bitches weren't worth lookin' at less we were sucking his dick. Jesus. So Roxie smiled and waved good-bye, but it wasn't right. It wasn't right. . . . Butch, Sierra's father, offered to keep her, but that seemed to terrify Roxie. She said that Tony wouldn't like that. He thought Sierra should only see her father on the days arranged as always, no exceptions. Butch got furious. He was the father. He'd see Sierra when he wanted. Then Roxie pleaded with him not to make so much of it. Then, she ran outside with Sierra. Butch went after them. Tony jumped out of the car. They had words. Butch came back in, real subdued. Butch told me there was nothing we could do but let her go.

——— He was right, you know.

——— Butch didn't want Roxie to die. God! He's Sierra's father. He didn't want the mother of his child to die. They were friends.

——— But even Roxie's friends couldn't stop her, Liliane.

——— Not her, Tony! Tony killed her! Why can't you accept that?

——— I'm not denying that Tony did this heinous crime, Liliane. I'm simply trying to help you accept that Roxie left herself and Sierra in very dangerous hands after repeated warnings from you and Butch, you see?

——— I was right in the first place. I told you I can't have therapy today. I just can't.

——— What do you want to do?

——— I want to shoot Tony. I want to kill him. I want to hurt him like he hurt Roxie and Sierra.

——— And you as well. Tony has hurt you too.

——— I want to see him dead.

——— Well, is he in custody?

——— Yes, of course, but he's pretending to be crazy. Son of a bitch.

——— Still, there'll be an arraignment, a trial.

——— Yes.
——— That's how things are done in this country, right?
——— Stop asking me questions! I'm not on trial here! He doesn't deserve a trial! He needs his eyes pulled from their sockets. I want to beat his skull with a baseball bat until there's nothing left but a pile of his filthy mean demented brain that long-haul trucks run over again and again so we can't even tell he was human.
——— Tony is human, Liliane.
——— No! No he isn't! He's an animal and he's alive and, and . . .
——— Roxie is dead.
——— I have to go home now. I have a lot of things to do. A memorial service, an inventory of paintings and sculptures, bank account. Roxie didn't have any family except Sierra, Butch, and me. That is all she had.
——— You all loved her very much, Liliane. That's a lot.
——— I'll call to reschedule. I'm not good at handling . . . death, you see.
——— Liliane, are you all right?
——— No. I'm not awright. I have to go home.
——— But, Liliane, you're walking toward the window, not the door.
——— Mommy. Mommy, don't leave me like this. Don't go! Don't go! Daddy, stop her! Please, Daddy, make her come home. Why are you standin' here like that? Mommy, Mommy, come back. Come back to me!

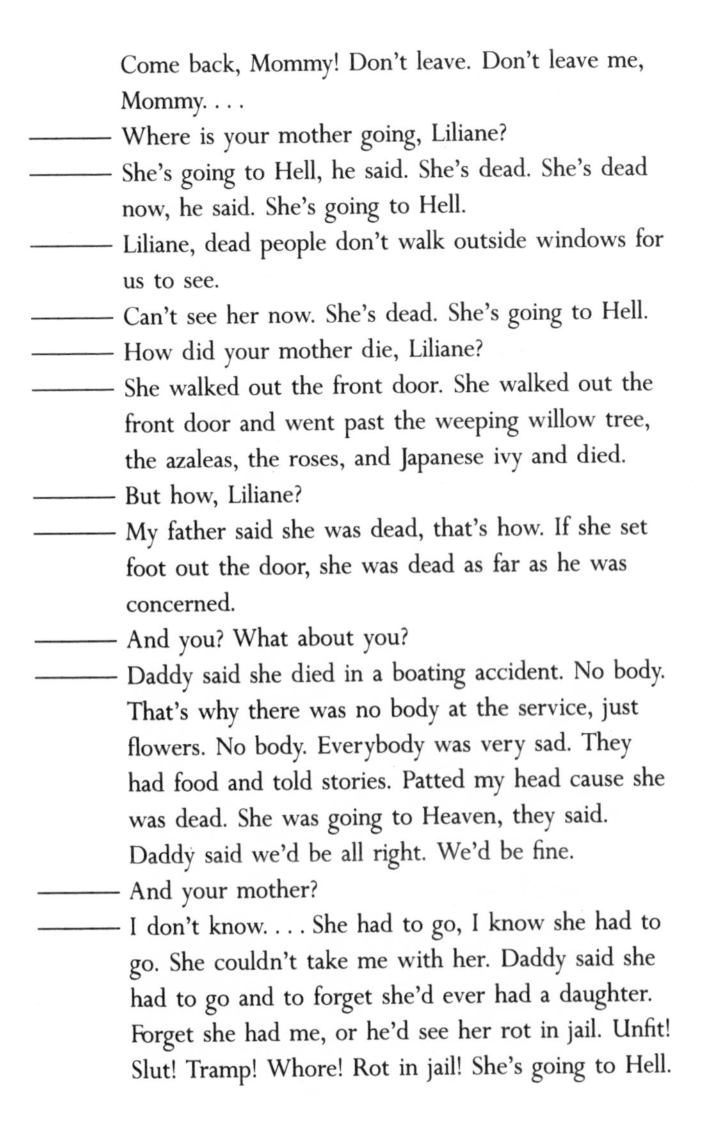

Come back, Mommy! Don't leave. Don't leave me, Mommy. . . .

——— Where is your mother going, Liliane?

——— She's going to Hell, he said. She's dead. She's dead now, he said. She's going to Hell.

——— Liliane, dead people don't walk outside windows for us to see.

——— Can't see her now. She's dead. She's going to Hell.

——— How did your mother die, Liliane?

——— She walked out the front door. She walked out the front door and went past the weeping willow tree, the azaleas, the roses, and Japanese ivy and died.

——— But how, Liliane?

——— My father said she was dead, that's how. If she set foot out the door, she was dead as far as he was concerned.

——— And you? What about you?

——— Daddy said she died in a boating accident. No body. That's why there was no body at the service, just flowers. No body. Everybody was very sad. They had food and told stories. Patted my head cause she was dead. She was going to Heaven, they said. Daddy said we'd be all right. We'd be fine.

——— And your mother?

——— I don't know. . . . She had to go, I know she had to go. She couldn't take me with her. Daddy said she had to go and to forget she'd ever had a daughter. Forget she had me, or he'd see her rot in jail. Unfit! Slut! Tramp! Whore! Rot in jail! She's going to Hell.

Mommy. Mommy, why didn't you take me! Mommy, Mommy, come get me, Mommy. Daddy said she's dead, she's dead. Better. Sluts can't raise children. Sluts run off with their lovers and die. They die and they can't take their children. I can't go with Mommy. She's dead. He said she was dead.

——— Is she, Liliane? Is your mother dead?

——— No, I don't think so. I don't know. She said not to worry. She said I'd understand, someday I'd understand. She couldn't live with my father anymore. She said she'd die if she stayed, if she stayed, she'd die. She went out the front door and died anyway. Oh, Jesus, you must really think I'm crazy now, huh?

——— No. You are making a lot of sense. If Roxie had done what your mother did, she might be alive now, like your mother.

——— My mother's been dead for years.

——— No. She's very much alive in you. She's helping you, even now.

——— Helping me, how's she helping me?

——— By reminding you of the window.

——— The window?

——— Yes. The window that opens to a world, worlds of beautiful trees and flowers and sunlight. A world full of life, Liliane.

——— But I'm not a part of it.

——— I beg to differ, Liliane. You are very much a part of it. If you need to call me for an emergency or just to chat, you know the number.

——— Could you, I know this is irregular, but do you think you could find the time to go see Roxie's show? It's the last of her we've got.

——— I think we should definitely talk some more about that, Liliane. Call, if you need me.

——— Yeah. I think I'll try the door this time. See you.

# Zoom Went the Strings of Liliane's Heart, But Arsenio Rodriguez Could Have Told Her the Music Sounds Just as Sweet When We're Blind and Still We See

From the top of this hill all of San Francisco sweeps into cascades of mist, strands of clouds and fog that fall through the sky and over the Bay like Iris Chacon's legs at the San Juan TV station. And those clouds came to dance with me over here, to mambo, to rhumba in a starlit wet night, but Puerto Rico is so far away. I walk the Mission lookin' every which way for a PR, any PR like me. Yeah, well, *compadre,* I hadta get back here before Lili censored herself into the company of devotées of *La Virgen de Guadalupe*. I mean, I'm not lettin' go of her one little bit, *mi corazón,* but she's gettin' headstrong, wants a limited relationship, equal responsibilities. And I cannot attempt to explain this drivel with any order or passion like the way she does.

*Mira,* the problem as I see it and know in my heart, which makes it a fact, is that my Lili has crossed over.

Now. I do not mean to say that *mi querida dulce* has in any way ever deserted her people or my people. I'm just meaning to suggest that this ridiculous affair she's havin' with this touchy-feely-lemme-talk-this-thru-witchu white boy is the reason I'm thinkin' bout layin' clouds steada layin' Lili. I mean, *hacer de amor con mi Liliane.*

*Cuidadate,* I say to her. When was the last time you heard about a "New White Man," *con los* Neanderthals, some Cro-Magnon guys roamin' Europe stark naked in snow. Hey, *tu sabe, negra,* that in the future, the future New White Man is still very white, *muy muy blanco en el universo sin los negros.* Now, whatchu think that portends, *corazón?*

But does she listen to me? Does she listen to me, the man whose heart beats to the *ritmo* of her breath, her stride, her, oh. Naw. She looks at me. Rolls my eyes, her eyes, my way. I don't understand. Oh, baby. The New White Man. The Old White Man. And a woman like you is the history of Puerto Rico. Damn. It's the history of the New World.

But she don't listen to me. She's not gonna run up here and tell you all about it, either. Her daddy would die. Ha, the New White Man. Her mother, *no te preocupe con ella;* she's on the other side, *gracias a Dios. Oigame.* I'm gonna tell you everything I know bout this romance with the Visigoths that Lili, awright, Liliane can't bring herself to reveal. Of course, she confided in me, cause, hey, I gotta way about me. I'm Victor-Jésus María.

I love her. I love her enough to tell you the truth no matter how much it hurts.

We know that notions come over women with the full moon or their periods or pregnancy. Women get cravings for good dick, or ice cream 'n pickles seems like in the natural course of the universe. But it never occurred to me, not ever, that Lili would getta yen for a biker. Now, don't you think that I woulda gone and found a motorcycle if I'd known my Lili was about to straddle a Harley that came with its own all-knowing white boy. Of course, I woulda. You know that. But see, I didn't get a chance. I didn't even know what I was up against.

Here we are working on Lili's new project: being the living tissue of lost ancestors in graves she digs along the Coast Highway where passing automobiles are flagged down to come to our funeral services which Lili officiates. We've got these feathers and cowries tied round our necks, faces painted, sometimes teeth, too. We are wrapped like mummies or simply in loincloths. Lili is sometimes naked with one flower over her navel. Anyway people get out of their cars and come to our funeral. Our spirits are nourished by their visits and the ghosts of the New World get up and dance with the *gringo* enthusiasts: That is until we reveal ourselves as the not-so-well-off folks of color from the Mission that we are. *Tu m'entiende* that dead Aztecs are so less threatening than a live *cholo.* Plus we gotta watch for the CHP, who don't take kindly to us digging up public property for graves of live niggahs.

*Mira,* I remember feeling like I don't want to die so young and handsome, plus, Lili had us singing Leadbelly's chain gang blues songs, while somebody else, Rosa I believe, went around chanting the rosary as a Franciscan friar in drag. It was, to say the least, very dirty work, the digging, getting ready to get in the holes we dug and then waiting for the visitors from this world. But whenever the sun leapt over the treetops like a golden jaguar's tongue licking fog off our skins and eyes and the cars would stop and follow Lili speaking Nauhlt directions, then I got off on the whole ceremony. Dead we ain't. Due ceremony and reverence, we are. I could get to that. *Estu bien, sus sueños de nuestra vida.*

I was grooving as the remains of a black Cherokee dressed as a buffalo soldier when this white boy who reminded me of flicks I've seen of General Custer, this white boy jumps off this Harley, leather jacket and all, to pay homage to the spirits of the New World. Now I only hear Lili's laughter and brisk deliberate steps, a "man's man" walking, when suddenly I am covered with sheet music, pages and pages of blank sheet music. Then, I hear Lili chanting some Yoruba elegy to a very out of tune Charlie Parker solo, circa 1948. *Qué pasa?* You know as well as I. The New White Man has put himself inside our piece, carved or seduced by an educated sleight-of-hand a role for himself. My Lili doesn't even move these papers off my face so I can get another glimpse at this interloper. She's laughing. A pale "April in Paris" stumbles from an archaic soprano sax in the hands of this Anglo, hair lying like black wings. From this position as a dead buffalo soldier, blank sheet music fluttering, a pair of old Doc Marten's by my graveside and a doomed melody sitting on the wind, I think to myself: This is too close to real life to be art.

And I was right, *tu sabe,* because Lili rode off on that bike with that white boy and what had been territory as yet undiscovered by European "explorers" was swept away on the wheels of a 750 Harley-Davidson. Now, I am not quick to anger, *yo say que yo tengo razón,* but I felt absolutely out of step, time, and my usual prowess this particular evening. After all I'm clad in nineteenth-century garb of a guy who terrorized Native Americans for a living on a hillside by the Pacific in the company of the son of Quetzal played by Winnie with blond dreads,

Sequoyah represented by Itami Kawakiya with orange braids, and Oya, the courtesan of Shango, in the person of Rosa when she is not a priest. Virtually beatified, we looked at one another in disbelief. Then Rosa became a priest again, said a blessing, and dismissed us to our real-life selves.

You have to admit what commitment I showed that day. Not leaving the site of the performance as this stranger rode off with *mi corazón*. I trust her. That's *muy facil, sí*. Oh, but even though I had warned Lili continually of the infinite paths to cultural compromise, I obviously had been duped.

By the time our truck was coming up the road from Guerneville with crackers reluctantly filling the tank of painted colored folks, Lili was nestled on the sands of Bolinas, a town without a sign so undesirables like us can't find it less we know somebody. Now, Lili knew somebody whose name was "Zoom." I kid you not. This was a white boy challenging the speed of light and sound, outdistancing those of us mired in primitive relics or nostalgia. Zoom went straight to Lili's heart. Who could resist a devotee to a process one is just inventing. *El proceso es la revolución. El proceso es todo.*

Lili likes to gloss over this part: the seduction by a white boy of *una negra* no white boy had touched, but how can we do that? This is of paramount significance, a departure from our realities that must be examined in detail, if we are to prevent its reoccurrence. *Entonces* we begin with this town that white people don't want us to know where it is: Bolinas. Clear uninterrupted waters, trees bosom branches sucking skies, Lili's ass caressing the surf with Zoom tween her legs. Oh, *dios mio,* I can hardly stand this, but I promised I'd tell the truth. She thought since she had never been with a white boy that it should accomplish some task, like she was in a fairy tale or something.

This is not my doing, I swear. Lili had this Zoom guy swimming tween her legs tryin' to kiss her clit in the water in the dark. Of course they both almost drowned. "But Victor, he tried," she squealed. Far as I'm concerned he lacks goddamned common sense or he would have told Lili that he could not and would not kiss her pussy floating in the water cause that seriously imperiled his life, but being the reformed and eager-to-please white boy that he is, he complied. Now, you see, the integrity of the fairy tale with Lili and Zoom defying the laws of physics allows them to skirt our cultural mores.

Yes, I realize I was not there with them at the time, in the moment to document their distortion of my sense of reality. *Pero,* I have photographed the location, the earthbound interstices of every single episode in Lili's chiaroscuro adventure; Zoom don't know what zoom is. I'm the reality test here. I take pictures in black and white that don't lie. Besides it's Lili who leaves traces of light wherever she's stepped or lain. She manifests as silver flashes on a two-dimensional plane. Still she talks to me:

"We spent the night on the beach by a small fire and wrapped in each other. I was a bit timid, kept imagining he thought me fast or loose like my grandma said all white men thought about us. I worried would he explore me like virgin timberland, Lewis and Clark of the avant-garde, or was I a performance piece of his. An unwitnessed happening. I checked to see if his neck was red. It wasn't. I sleep soundly."

That's not all they experienced together, a common dream, a common sweat raspy with inarticulate spurious desire. Zoom turns out to have a name, Joel, given him by his white parents who always told him to be nice to everybody, especially the "Negroes," whose life was so hard.

"I don't need you to be nice to me, goddamn you. We've never needed white people to do anything for us, let alone be nice to us. And just what was your poor white trash ass gonna do for me anyway? Huh? Teach me about what? Lincoln and Bix whatever his name is? This isn't going to work. It's not even a sane activity. Why didn't you just play your little tune, get on your bike and go wherever white men go after they've been somewhere they don't belong?"

"Listen to yourself, Liliane," Zoom firmly but softly utters the first words of his pattern of seduction that keeps my Lili constantly reevaluating the immediate effects of racism on her and her loved ones. "Listen to yourself, Lili," like that was going to absolve him of any association with the bloody limits of our expectations and hopes dashed on barbed wire and ropes. With the charm of Dave Brubeck and the guts of Stan Getz he wound his way through Lili's perceptions, changing lenses constantly, reframing her instincts, her sense of touch. If she held him tentatively, with caution, that was her own racism keeping her from him. When she heard nothing in Steve Lacy's escapades, she had closed herself off. If Paul Whiteman was not the King of Jazz, she didn't know that music has no boundaries, is a gift, is universal. Humph, just a ball of confusion, my Lili, *mi corazón*.

"Victor-Jésus, do you know there are some of us who have gone off with some of them and we never see each other?" I didn't understand.

"No, really, Victor, we went to a cove where this barn had

been done over for performances and a gallery. It was so pristine and free of clutter, not like alternative spaces in the city. All these other white people, artists, Zoom claims, owned this place and lived out there. I said, 'Well, okay.' I chatted with some women who run a shelter and some others who make chapbooks, and it was like grade school. A bunch of white people who are not necessarily dangerous, but still alien, whose faces I wouldn't remember, or names. I was getting fidgety, wanting to go somewhere I mattered, when this black guy with dreadlocks appeared from nowhere, like an extraterrestrial. But, and this is the weird thing, he looked at me like I had done something to him. He's the only other one of us there. He was colder than the white people whose names I don't remember."

Me, of course, I say nothing, *nada.* Who am I to judge? Yet I was not alone having a hard time watching Lili cavort thru the Fillmore, even the Point, on the back of this Harley holding on to a till-the-death cracker. This is when her extraterrestrial aspects loomed, but she didn't notice. A couple of brothers at the corner of Divisadero near Scott threatened to pour oil on the road, if they came back that way. All they really had to do was wash out the Jerri-Curl. But their instincts were on the mark, *compadre.* Right on the mark.

Lili took to wearing a beret when she and Zoom were about town. She even invited him to a few more ceremonies and parties that our little group had now and again. Zoom mingled well, like he'd been waiting all his life to not be so white, to be comfortable when he was the only one of them around in a way that Lili could not. I assume this is a privilege of race, but don't let me sway you. From Tower of Power to Larry Graham, even Tito Puente's *ritmo* couldn't contain Zoom's exuberance when he was dancing. The whole world was at risk with his gangly out-of-control I-am-a-white-boy contortions. After he knocked over a lamp and a few glasses of wine and stepped on Kim Sheang's toes two times, Lili indignantly led him away. He didn't want to leave, poor thing, having such a good time cavortin' with the natives.

"Where are you going?" Zoom inquired.

"Home. I'm going home."

"Hop on, then." He straddled his other black sweetheart and revved up. "Get on, I said."

Now Zoom didn't look so friendly, eager to please.

"Victor-Jésus, how can I tell you? He looked mean like any other mean white man, but it passed really quickly. We went over to La Rondallo for some quesadillas and sangria. The Mariachis sang 'Guadalajara' for me. He pulled out his clarinet and we romped through the Mission for hours. When we're alone, I think, this guy is great. He's so free and gentle, most of the time, anyway."

I am considering the various cleansing rituals to which Lili must submit before I can take her back from this latest *conquistador,* but the intrigue has not yet peaked. Lili thinks I'm quaint. A remnant of precultural diversity socialization, like her father, maybe.

"I decided to tell Daddy that Zoom, I mean, Joel, is just a very, very light, light black man."

I laughed so hard I had to pee and get a *cerveza.* A light light black man. Not to upset Daddy's life spectrum, to leave the family image intact, to make believe it doesn't matter, to lie. Lili. Lili, to lie to a good white lay. *Querida,* you can do better than that, I say.

"You shouldn't laugh at me, Victor-Jésus."

"*Tu queres que yo lioro para ti,* you want me to weep, *mija?*"

"You almost had to. Victor-Jésus, it was so scary. He was so scary."

What's scary about clumsy white men is beyond me but I listen.

"I was lying on the water bed at my house. It was dark and light at once cause of the fog. We were just about inside clouds, close to heaven. I felt so cherishd. Zoom had licked me all over, I was shivering and warm, and moist."

"Yes, Lili . . ."

"Well, I told Zoom that I'd sent my father some photos of us together, that I'd painted over his face and arms so they would look darker. I didn't want any trouble with Daddy, you know. I thought he'd understand. We don't have and have never had, since slavery, any white folks in the family. . . . Well. He changed. Victor, he stomped around my house like some interrogator from a grade B movie. He screamed at me. 'Nobody has the right to be ashamed of me. You have no right to make me dark or light or less white. Who do you think you are, you bitch.'

"Then, I don't know how I got there. I was in the kitchen with a butcher knife. I was looking at my Zoom, saying, 'You get out of my house now. Get out right now.' He looked bewildered. I said, 'Zoom, get out now before I try to hurt you. Get out.' I screamed. I started to cry but my hand didn't waver. I held the knife in front of me toward the door til I heard him start up the bike. Then I knew how primitive I am. Victor, I couldn't have a white man, not even Zoom, raise his voice to me in my house. I just couldn't."

Ha. And you thought she wasn't my girl.

"Every single word, every step he took toward me, became somewhere else, somebody else, another white man, out of his place, any white man putting himself in my life where he didn't belong, had no rights. I looked at Zoom, my Zoom, the black curls dancin' over his eyes, but he wasn't there. Only a snarlin' mouth with white trash beard crowdin' his lips kept circlin' me. I had to do somethin'. This is my house. This isn't the Highway Five or Alabama, or Chambersburg. I'm the one who makes the rules in my house. White people just can't walk in and turn everything upside down, make me not belong to me again. He was just everywhere. Oh, he's shouting for me to listen to what he's sayin'. I don't haveta listen to shit. I've heard every goddamned idea any white man ever had. I've heard it all awready. He musta lost his mind. Well, I showed his stupid white ass. If a niggah bitch is what he was after, a niggah bitch gone fuckin' crazy is what he muthafuckin' got. Jesus, my grandma must be rollin' in her grave. Lord, what am I gonna do? What can I do now to be rid of this mess? Shit. How could this happen? How could this happen to me? How did I do this? I've gotta take responsibility for myself, I know. How am I gonna get that fuckin' cracker voice outta my house? How am I gonna get him off me? His hands and tongue, his arms. He usedta lift me til my head touched the ceilin'. 'We were goin' to reach the foothills of Heaven,' he said. 'We were. That nothin' and nobody was going to stop us.' "

It's not funny, but Lili was pale as a sheet *como* the Breck girl. As carefully as I could I swallowed my laughter, actual hoots, *gritas en realidad.* Somebody put an end to all her madness for sure. And those somebodies sure didn't take no instructions from *El Señor Zoom,* either. "In the foothills of Heaven," *coño.* The steppes of Hades is more like where he and his kind ended up with Malinche, holograms of the Venus Hottentot, multitudes of writhing Negress wenches leaping from mahogany bedsteads and barn rafters. "The foothills of Heaven." I noticed that Lili was cryin', not weeping, but having tears, quiet.

"Was it worth it?" I asked softly.

"What—what do you mean?" Lili stammered slowly, breathless like she'd escaped with her life.

"You don't understand, Victor. Zoom was always so nice to me. He was so gentle and he made me feel . . ." Lili stopped, bit her lower lip with her two front teeth. I knew what that signaled. That was Lili's physical gesture for visceral memories of orgasmic ecstacies which meant I didn't haveta wear the kid gloves anymore. I mean, I have limits too.

Lili was randomly filling pages of newsprint with what I took to be those fuckin' black ringlets of the former white boy lover, Zoom, at every angle, I guess. Her eyes reached for me and then dashed away into the charcoal swirls away from me.

"Liliane." She didn't look at me. "Liliane," I said again more firmly. "Did he ever use the word 'cunt' in your presence?" I didn't wanta ask if he ever called her that or if he pulled gently at her vulva and whispered how pretty her cunt was, what a beautiful cunt she had. She was, my Lili, *mi querida.*

"Well, did he ever use the word 'cunt'?"

"Why? Why do you want to know that? What's that for?"

Though philological and semantic intercourse had never fazed her before, now Lili was stumped. "What are you talkin' about?" she repeated over and over.

His scalp, those goddamned curls, I wanted his scalp like

Pontiac and Hatuey had demanded. The back of my mouth was viciously sour and clamped my breath back toward my heart pumping vengefully.

"I want to know the extent of the violation, Lili. That's all. In a word, 'cunt.' "

I could see each letter, c-u-n-t, rip through Lili's bosom like the knife she'd wielded in her kitchen. I knew this hurt. I knew that, but Lili needed to know that what hurt wasn't her emboldened stance to protect herself; her resort to force, to violence, wasn't the sad revelation of the hour. It was Zoom's ease within his whiteness, his presumptuous colonization of my Lili's spirit, body. Lili succumbed, in the end, to too great an optimism, a naïveté fed by Zoom's awkward attempts to move smoothly in the throng of our worlds, like the priests and union organizers; he wanted to get to know us. Ever gracious, Lili led the way. Now she was afraid. She knew she couldn't always see the danger. She followed the wrong instincts. She'd lain still, smilin', while some white boy explored her, droppin' filthy lil words over her most sacred places.

"*Mira, querida,* Liliane. *No te preocupe.*" I sang to her. "Let's go take a bath." Lili's eyes filled her cheeks, pulled her full lips to a grin. Her strange laughs tickled me behind my ears, crawled up my chin into my mouth where I nestle them, single giggles under my tongue.

We were whole again, were going to be soon at any rate. The thing that Lili said that assured me she had learned her lesson was watching her skip backward down Valencia, throwin' kisses to me between quotes from Gylan Kain: "Shoulda cut the muthafuckah, made him bleed."

# Room in the Dark VII

——— You know I might get married?
——— No. Actually, I did not.
——— Well, goes to show, you never know who knows.
——— Does that mean that in addition to my not knowing that you were getting married, that I also don't know something else that's important to you?
——— Who's to say what's important to you? Like you don't know?
——— You give me a lot of credit here, Liliane.
——— Is it you calling my actual name or what you don't know should impress me?
——— Right now, an answer, even a response, to either would satisfy me.
——— Who said anything about satisfyin' your behind, tell

me that? Who said it and where is he? You want to know what I wanta know, that's it. That's it.

——— Who do you think told me, Liliane?

——— See, that's it. I can't deal with this anymore. I told you I was gettin' married and you gonna act the fool.

——— I thought we were getting married nine years after your treatment ended. So your life would be full and effective and I would not lose my license.

——— You remember too many things.

——— That's my job, I think. No. I know that, but what'd be more interesting is what you think.

——— You must be dreamin'.

——— No. Actually I've had no dreams lately.

——— I have.

——— Really. You have in the last few days?

——— Yes. Oh, yes, can I tell you one?

——— Well, you know, Liliane, I'm at your service.

——— Yeah, fifty minutes a week, muthafuckah.

——— Well, do you really want to marry me?

——— Hell, no. That's more than a lifetime commitment. That's my mother and my father and their mothers and fathers all sayin' that they in love with you.

——— Well, isn't that a reasonable possibility?

——— No. You too dark.

——— Cause I'm Creole, Liliane.

——— Who would know that?

——— Well, I'm supposing that your family'd know every possible reason they won't want you to marry me.

I'm shiftless, I'm brutal, I'm ignorant; I'm stupid; I'm clumsy; I was born on the left side of the bed.

——— No, that would help. My grandma always said chirren born on the left side of the bed brought God's bounty. Niggah, what in the fuck are you talkin' bout?

——— Whether I am your curse or your dream?

——— And so? You know my mommy married that awful white man and took his name S. Bliss Rothenstein as if me and Daddy had never existed?

——— What does that have to do with us?

——— Sometimes I think you are really with me. Then I turn around and you are just another stupid muthafuckah.

——— But how could I know that, Liliane. You say I am too smart and turn round and say I'm dumb . . . That I'm here and not here? I can understand everything about you and I can't?

——— Can we really talk about my dream?

——— Of course.

——— But I don't mean my "dreams," I mean a dream I had.

——— Fine.

——— No. I mean, don't screw me around. For alla my life my "dream" has been to marry into one of those families like my family and end up idiots with some land and titles.

——— What has that to do with your dream?

——— Well, nothing, actually.

——— Liliane, I am getting the definite impression that your dreams are being forced into somebody else's "dream" who has nothing to do with us.

——— Anybody black has something to do with us.

———

———

——— Is everybody else in your dream?

——— No, but . . .

———

——— Okay, I'll tell you. In an apartment I live in with Thayer in Paris, 17th Arrondissement with an android who has three faces and a woman who has two behinds like a table, I have a wonderful esplanade. Yet outside my apartment I see Thayer burying a million dollars and waving at me like our future is assured, but the android with eyes that became neon whenever he spoke and his eyes lit up was restless. He said, "Oh yes, it's just that Thayer doesn't know where he's buried the money." With this I start to panic, but the android, whose name is Pratt, says I shouldn't be worried cause they've awready started looking for it. I look out over the esplanade, which is quite large, to see Thayer digging.

Hyacinthe says I should go along with her because it'll take forever for them to find this million dollars. So we start to walk through all the rooms which are very airy with floor-to-ceiling windows and parquet floors. After what seems like a terribly long journey through the bright and wide rooms, we come to an arch of marble. We go through this arch into a bustlin' Pan-African market. Everybody from Fez to Nairobi or Dakar had items for sale or was buying. But the currency was cruzeiros, which puzzled me, but also took some of the sting out of my situation. I couldn't feel too badly about not having cruzeiros because my million dollars was buried somewhere in front of my apartment. And we don't even know where that was.

Hyacinthe and I look at a lot of things at the market. Yet I am attracted to a woman with a stall where fossilized woods and stones were joined to crystal hand-hewn pieces. There are several that I like and I tell her I'll be back.

——— Yes, Lili . . . What do you make of that?

——— Oh, there's a bit more. . . .

——— Okay.

——— We went all the way back to the apartment and Hyacinthe was going on and on about some revolt in the Côte d'Ivoire. She kept talking and I kept thinking about all that old, old wood, older than Jesus, older than Charlemagne or Sundiata. I want some of that. I wanted something like me.

When we got back to our flat, I discover the entire esplanade has been torn apart by Thayer, Pratt the android with three faces, and the super, who's named Sawyer.

Like all guys, they see the alarm on my face and laugh. They've found the million dollars awready and will fix my esplanade back to its original state or any state I desire.

Then I start to tell Thayer about the stones and the crystals I saw; that the woman in the African market expects my return. Thayer smiles that we don't need to go that far. He summons the woman with two backsides, Susi, who leads down a hallway to a locked door that she has a key for. "I'm the only one can do this. You can't get in this door without me. No. No. No. Without me, no entry."

I go into the room. I discover that all the objects including the furniture are made of carved Lalique with the same sort of curvature as the jewelry in the market. I remember that she had said to me that she always left a signature on any piece she and her husband executed. It was an antelope in the midst of a leap of some kind. She always kept everything asymmetrical. I looked a bit more closely at the crystalline couches, found her sign, and was content.

——— That's a deliciously ornamental dream, Lili.

——— It's about a house.

——— But what a house it is! It leads from this world to another; has a three-headed android who is sensitive to your needs; a two-backsided woman who is willing to share her secret, and a man who's going to dig up your garden in Métro-Paris, find a million dollars, tell you he found it, and put your garden back however you want. . . .

——— Yes, and then there's the African woman with crystal and antelope signs. . . .

——— And she didn't even have to make anything for you.
——— Why not? What's wrong with me?
——— Nothing, Liliane.
——— Then what are you talking about?
——— Even in your dreams the floors you walked, the couches you sat in, the bed you made. All these were . . .
——— What? Used, had awready, dirty, what?
——— I was going to say what I really believe. The rooms in your dream, just like everything else, but especially your bed and your tables and floors were precious.
——— Really.
——— It was a marvelously optimistic and beautiful dream, Liliane.
——— Yeah?
——— It's time.
——— I know, whenever I start to feel good. "It's time."
——— You may be right about that.
——— I know how to fix you. "I'll see you in my dreams."

# I Know Where the E Train Stops
# But
# I'm "Sendin' Out an S.O.S."
# and
# I'm Not Edwin Starr Either

One thing for sure was Cadwalder Creek was nothing like Baisley Lake in Queens. I mean, for one thing there's benches and trees, tennis courts, and a promenade that goes all the way around the water just how the boardwalk straddles Asbury Park or Atlantic City, but without the hawkers and trash. Then, of course, there's no ocean. Now I've been down South where my folks are from; even went to Rehoboth one time. But see, comin' to Baisley Park was, well, real excitin' cause there was more colored people like Liliane and her daddy.

I always thought that whole bunch was strange, but I liked to fell out laughin' when I heard the good judge was sendin' Liliane to Queens to get away from us. Wasn't her fault or nothin', but your kin can't be puttin' way everybody's relations and expect kindly reactions. Hell, he would have been after me, but I was a friend of Danny's, which meant I was a friend of Liliane's too, in some kind of way. Of course, I never took advantage of all this favor and do, but I know Danny and Liliane was looking for me to even up the score on the favors I done did for her ass. Seems like to me that with all the experiences and folderol spent on the girl that she'd add up to something more than she was, but I ain't never really been nowhere, so who am I to say. But lemme tell you how we got to Baisley Park in the first place. Humph, I need to remind myself sometimes how peculiar colored folks' lives really are.

We was at the Trenton train station waiting on my big sisters to come in from Newark, when I saw Liliane and her mama waiting for the same train. I didn't know if they was going someplace or was bidin' time or what. Lotsa folks was at the boarding platform waitin', cause this was the last night of Girls Carnival over to the high school. Now a town built round a mess of factories and run by folks who learned the word "niggah" the same time they learned how to say, "Gimme a coke, please," is not weighed down with civic rituals. But for most forty years, maybe a lil more, maybe a lil less, Girls Carnival had thrown all the nastiness and bickering between real white folks and new white folks, colored and Puerto Ricans to the sidelines, leaving the girls to compete on one of two teams: either White or Blue. By the time I came around, generations of my aunts, cousins, and my mama had been consumed by Blue passions. A girl would just as soon thought about marrying a cracker as considering being White Team. This is the absolute truth.

Don't laugh, but it's my understanding that Liliane's mama told her to see which team had the most niggahs on it, then choose to join the other one. That's the reason, accordin' to my sources, that Liliane was the White Team color bearer. She couldn't do any of the specialty routines cause it was "too common." Only reason she was in the public high school at all, far as I could tell, was cause the private ones close by didn't take no kinda colored folks. So here was Liliane's poor mama, looking afflicted every time her child gushed a "Hello, how ya doin'?" to the colored riffraff waitin' on the train. I mean, the woman tried to be convivial and all, but the small of her back ached so her shoulders was half a foot behind her head, and her lips curled up so tight I thought she must be sucking a lemon to be so mince-mouthed in all this excitement.

My sister, Patsy, and my cousins Margie and Flo come off the train belting Blue Team cheers: "We blue Blue Team girls are hot for sho'/Throw the White Team gals right thru the flo'." I was so happy to see them. I didn't really notice Liliane greeting her friend, girl's name was Rose Lynne or something like that. She was from Baisley Park, come to see Liliane bear the White Team flag which was a hoot cause she was gonna bear it in defeat. Now, that's the truth.

But first Liliane and Rose Lynne got my friend Danny in a heap of trouble. Him just trying to be nice to his honey and all. See, Liliane didn't want to be on no White Team no more than she wanted to drop dead, but she didn't have the backbone to stand up for herself. Once Rose Lynne scoped the deal, she convinced Liliane to stop frontin' and let the other colored people know she was forced to be a White Team girl. That way, she and Rose Lynne could still have a great time at the Victory Dance for the Blue Team.

The score was 53–27; Blues ahead. Like I said the Whites were gonna eat the dust, like they oughtta. So less they won everything: Modern Dance, Jazz, Folk, Gymnastics, and Acrobatics, they might as well have stayed home. Ha! Danny's mama and his cousins' mamas was all Blue Team, too, so he couldn't have gone to a White Team any kinda party without folks thinkin' he was pussy-whipped. Now I'm not sayin' I know for truth, but I think Mrs. Lincoln locked that child's brain and pussy somewhere in her house til wasn't no more niggahs on the planet. Anyway, Danny and Rose Lynne convinced Liliane that she was going to the Blue Team party for three reasons: 1) her boyfriend's folks was Blue; 2) Rose Lynne wanted to meet Danny's cousins; 3) Liliane didn't wanta associate with losers who were the White Team. Simple.

The Judge had finally let Danny come visit Liliane in his home cause, much to his surprise, Danny was an industrious son of a bitch. Danny worked as a caddy at the golf course by the Judge's home where, guess what, the Judge could not play golf unless he was some white lawyer's guest. See, the Judge showed up on the green with his golf bag and all, justa huffin' and puffin'. The other caddies had run like lap dogs to their reg'lar white men, but Danny he laid back. Then he offered his services to the Judge with a real twinkle in his eye. Now the Judge knew that Danny didn't boot-lick no white man. That was enough pedigree for the Judge, but not for his wife. She tagged along on all their so-called dates like she was one of them women in "Zorro" sent by the king to look after the booty. Still, alla this contributed to the success of the plan; to skip out of the gym and get to the Blue Team party before Liliane's mama could figure out anything, 'cept that the girls was with Danny and Danny was a nice Negro fellow trying to better himself. Who could ask for anything more?

Well, the Whites were clobbered 76–27 on the last nite. All

the screams of Faye Wray and Godzilla would have been whimpers compared to how we was hootin' that night. Lemme tell you, all Danny could do to get through the crowd to me was to elbow them girls like they was as tough as they wanted to be. Danny gets up next to me whispering, "Bernadette, I need you to get Liliane and her friend Rose Lynne into the Blue Team party. Can you do it?" Now, has Bernadette Reeves ever been unable to do something she set her mind to? Naw. So I turn round, best I can in a crowd: "Danny, put em in your car in they party dresses, not no White Team mess. Get Liliane to put some more makeup on and fluff that other child's hair round her face, so they don't draw attention. Then, wait for me by the door on the Evans Street side." Soon as the words was out my mouth, Danny was nigh behind the wheel of his car; Rose Lynne pullin' Liliane with her to some real live colored fun. I could tell by the look in her eyes at the station. She wanted to know what went on with us after her folks, like Liliane's, looked us over at the door and turned us away with one glance at the security guard. Off we went, all dressed up and turned away at the ball, you get what I'm sayin'? Yeah, that Rose Lynne wanted a peek at the forbidden: Negroes off guard, Negroes she was guarded from. Now, this was not gonna to be hard, at all. The Blues was on fire with the delight of triumph; the giddiness of spiked punch and swigs of 151 proof rum in backseats of low-ridin' overloaded Chevies; choruses of Tina Turner imposters shoutin' from car to car, all the windows down, cars switching lanes like a Little Anthony swirls capes to the tune "I'm Blue-ooh-ooh-ohohoh/Hey/Hey/tell me now/ now what'd I say/I'm Blue/ooh-ooh-ooh . . ." all back up into the town where the party was. P.A.R.T.E.E.

And we were sharp, I'm sayin'. They was girls with they hair ratted least seven inches in the air with these danglin' lost-lookin' Shirley Temple curls on the sides of they faces. Guys witih do's bad as Jackie Wilson's, decked out in silk suits and soft foreign leather dancin' slippers. You could almost smell the new on everybody, besides they sweat. Fancy-ass-footwork, crinolines pullt way past knees, bosoms bouncin' far as Bristol, gotta holdt of the 'burg that night. We was high. We was silly. We gotta-gettin-to-a-go-go and forgot bout blocks and blocks of guineas only wanted niggahs to get gone, get lost, get dead quick as a pipe'll break glass.

And dontcha know with one door bein' broke down, glass crashin' everywhere, and girls shriekin' til they had no more breath, any niggah thought she was on a Blue Team sho' stepped fast to a black one. We wasn't fightin' no White Team now. We was up against a mess of race-crazed crackers who couldn't hold pencils no better'n us or read faster or talk clearer; just some white trash defendin' what lil they knew they had: a bunch of nasty lil streets with nasty lil relatives of Paul Anka and Fabian tendin' to em. But shit, we couldn't kick ass like we was accustomed. I'm in my heels, five inches and a dress too tight to waddle. Alla that came off cause I wasn't havin' no guinea jump bad with me and not pay. I'm pullin' my arm back to swing into this Funicello-lookin' bitch, when Danny comes shoutin': "We gotta get Liliane outta here." I know that boy had lost his brains up in that hincty gal's crotch, but hell we all hadta get outta there. It was like in the movies. You know, how the saloon girls get up next to the wall like the wall's gonna protect em? I saw Liliane and that Rose Lynne tryin' to climb over and thru folks who was lookin' like bloody messes gone completely wild. Those two didn't hide they faces or crouch over to stop off punches. It was pathetic. But me thinkin' bout them, just set me up for some real fool guinea gal decided to pull my head off my neck. Well, once I threw her ass over a table, I moved my behind over to the wall where the simple-assed Liliane and her friend was tryin' to follow Danny out to the street.

Don't ask me how I knew, but I was sure the street was more terrible than the dance hall. It was the crackers' territory. They neighborhood and like that. Shit. Somebody shoulda brought some guns. Don't matter if you a Blue or a White Team girl, if you black in the 'burg you outta bounds and I'm black if I'm alive and I swear for Jesus I wasn't bout to meet my maker in the 'burg and I wasn't bout to risk my behind lookin' out for two bitches couldn't fight as good as po' white trash. Who did they think they were? They don't haveta know how to do nothin' bout theyselves? Shit. I pushed that Rose Lynne gal on her ass so fast she was happy to hold on to that ol' tree root. Danny shoved Liliane behind him, when this crowd of white boys started runnin' toward us, shoutin': "Get them niggahs." Liliane tried to stand up with one shoe on, the other broke in her hand. I pulled her down on top of me just as this cracker fool whipped a chain above our heads. We just crawled and kicked and moaned toward the curb til I saw Flo, my cousin, backin' her car up with the doors open in the back. I shouted to Danny; "Hey, we gotta book now, man." Then I smacked that Rose Lynne bitch: "Get in the car, fool." "But, it's movin'," she says. "It's movin', the car is movin'," I'm thinkin' to myself. Then, I realize Liliane's runnin' in the wrong direction. She thinks Flo is tryin' to get her. I go after Liliane.

Flo rears the car back toward us more, but there's more guineas back this way. Danny throws Rose Lynne in the backseat. Liliane hears us callin' her finally. I grab her arm as she gets close enough, we try to jump for the car, but some greasy ducktail fool get holdt of Liliane's ankle and won't let go. I shout to Patsy, tell Flo to keep the car movin', don't stop or we are some dead colored people. Danny's climbin' over Rose Lynne's sobbin' body, tryin' to help me, but I can't tell who's talkin' to me. Liliane's swingin' on the pavement like a bunch of tin cans at somebody's wedding, but the sounds she makin' ain't hardly no tinklin's of joy. I tell her to kick the muthafuckah off her. Just kick. *Kick* I tell her.

Well, she musta done somethin' I tol' her cause she whirled up into the backseat like a rubberband, she did. Slammed the door shut. Flo put her foot to the floor. And we was outta there. A bunch of bruised, bloody niggahs, some tore-up lookin' niggahs, smellin' of fresh wounds and cheap wine, but we wasn't dead. I gotta say that. We was alive. And Liliane's been sort of my friend ever since. See, she ain't much to me at all. I always figured she was some other kinda white girl. Now, I'm not talkin' bout Girls Carnival here. I'm sayin' that it wasn't nothin' personal, but she and girls like her and Rose Lynne were due about the same respect you'd give a mangy dog what couldn't fend for itself. I wouldn't let her know that now, I'm not a mean person. But, believe me, we did not go through something together. We was just at the same place. We wasn't in nothin' together.

But here I am in Baisley Park with Liliane and Rose Lynne. Special invitation to some nighttime barbecue where there won't be no guineas, no chains, no guns. No people like me to turn away.

Danny made me promise not to tell Liliane that he was plannin' on comin' to this affair in Queens whether she was gonna tell him about it or not. I memorized what we did once we got off the E train on the Independent line and caught the Q-44 bus. Now down by the subway stop looked like the movies for real. There were overhead rail lines for some other kinda trains went to Brooklyn. Big old blue steel pillars comin' right up the sidewalks far as I could see. All these stores, piles of people comin' from underneath the cement. I almost wanted to turn right around and go back to New Jersey. I'd heard that boys and girls actually made dates on the subway with people they'd just met or saw everyday at the same time on the same platform. Danny was to take this E train to Sutphin Boulevard and wait on the bus just like we did. I wasn't real convinced this was a good idea, now, but Danny was my buddy. When we got really going on the Q-44, I couldn't stop looking out the windows. So many colored people going in and out these houses that was standing on they own, not attached, you know. Here I was in New York City and there was trees taller than the bus, too. I saw a little house with gray round stones, the kind they used to make field markers with, had a fish pond in the front with a mer-man or a boy-fish leanin' over the water, I thought maybe there should be some of them like black jockey boys holdin' they hands out in front of some of these places, but then since real little Negro boys lived in these houses, wasn't no need to pay for fake ones. Rose Lynne occasionally waved out the window to this or that grown-up. Was this being polite, a way of stayin' out of trouble, or settin' up these pedestrians for some scheme, I wondered.

Once we was near the party, I knew it. Music was all up in the air long with roasting okra and broiling meat. Liliane heard it, too. I leaned over to her to say we must be gettin' close, but she didn't act like herself. I thought I might talk to Rose Lynne, but her mind was definitely between her legs by this time. I could tell cause she was taking these very slow deep breaths and openin' and closin' her eyes like there was something caught on her eyelash. Well, I knew how to perform well as them two. I started fondlin' my fingers how I'd seen my mama 'fore she went out, like I was stretchin' my nails by my willpower.

I don't know bout you, but I can always tell when I'm not wanted. I didn't have no trouble readin' tween the lines, lookin' at the faces of the mothers of these kids, goin' up and down my body like some niggah disease was goin' to slip off me or my shorts onto their precious children. Do the black come off faster if your Daddy does day labor? That's what I shoulda asked them. No matter, though. Liliane and Rose Lynne was just a-huggin' and kissin' this one and that one, sayin' this is Bernadette from Jersey as they went along. Didn't hardly speak to no boys which is why I wanted to be at the joint. Anyway, they didn't look so different from other colored folks I'd seen and grown up with, but there was something different: could have been how the girls' hair didn't go back, or the way they looked straight ahead of themselves all the time like there wasn't no danger nearby. At first I thought the difference was how a bunch of foreign words dropped out they mouths between hugs and kisses, but I'm not sure. Liliane seemed to have begun to stand up straighter like something was at stake here. She moved her head from one side to the other real slow with her eyes wide open and her mouth set very serious. I hoped I could tell her Danny was on his way right behind us before she spotted him, looking about so hard the way she was. But, ain't I slow.

Before I could get my mouth set to whisper about Danny's plan to surprise her, Liliane ran into the arms of this fella was made of gold, I swear. I never saw no colored boy move like folks should leave him alone unless he was dangerous, you know, packin'. This fella walked cross the patio, past the silver fountain spoutin' punch and the pink balloons and rose bushes like he owned them, but he was visitin' just like me. Liliane jumped down from his arms. He must have been six feet if he was an inch. She grabbed his hand, come rushin' over to me, sayin': "Bernadette, this is Granville Simeon, a very dear friend of mine." Well, you know, I could tell how much a friend this Granville was by the way they was leanin' and touchin' on each other. Lord, Danny was in for a helluva night.

This Granville had a English accent made me think he was a West Indian or a Negro what put on airs, but he was smooth, I gotta say that. He was more friendly to me than the rest of these people, especially nicer than the Negroes servin' the food was. Here they was in they little bonnets and aprons, big-grown folks, waitin' on teenagers black as them who took no notice of them, like the trays was just sittin' on air and goin' bout the yard on they own. Oh, but when they got to me, didn't they eyes just roll this way and that like I was a serious mistake and if they rolled they eyes far enough to one side, by the time they eyes got back to where they could see in front of them I'd be gone. But I was there, smilin', and waitin' for someone to ask me to dance.

And with all the fancy carryin' on, these Negroes could still move with style, I'll say that. I was dancin', too. Although I thought I might be a bit much for the way this boy was shufflin' his feet, at least I was on the floor. Yes, I was. His name was Roy somethin'. He was soft-spoken and tall, smelled good. I saw Rose Lynne run off behind this little house next to the garage. Hum. Then I saw Liliane waving her hand at me, mouthing that she was just checkin' to see I was havin' a good time. I was feelin' more like an explorer, you know, than actually enjoyin' myself. I wanted to remember everythin' so I could tell my friends in Jersey what all these Negroes was up to. I know cause I could tell that Liliane and Granville was a hot match. Nobody paid them no mind which means they attempts to grind into each other with they clothes on was an ordinary sight. I hoped Danny had missed the bus or got lost or somethin'.

Next thing I know Rose Lynne come runnin' out the bushes in tears, sobbin' and holdin' her head down. Now hadn't one of these acne-free polished Negroes held they head down all evenin', so I thought that fella musta shamed Rose Lynne which is what happens when you go in the bushes with a fella anyway. Liliane broke way from Granville, fine as his black ass was, to tend to Rose Lynne. I excused myself from Roy, I know my manners, too, you see. Then I went right behind them.

Liliane was holdin' Rose Lynne's head on her lap, caressin' her hair and rockin' her back and forth. I thought the boy must have been drafted or somethin', like her mother was dyin' or his mother was dyin'. Liliane looked up at me with a look I'd seen on the faces of the ladies of the house. What was I doin' there. I pulled my breath back into my body so my hands wouldn't embarrass me and asked them what was wrong. Liliane gritted her teeth. "That jerk, Ronnie, hurt her feelings, that's all." I looked real hard. Rose Lynne cried with more thrashin' of her bosom. Then, she raised her head defiantlike and held her hand out suddenly: "Look at this. Look at this." Rose Lynne bent over Liliane's lap again, her arm danglin' from her body and in her hand was a beautiful gold ring with a green stone and diamonds on each side. "Why that's beautiful, Rose Lynne."

Liliane shook her head silently like I should be quiet. Rose Lynne shouted, "No, no," between gasps for air. What in the devil was wrong with these girls, I asked myself. Suddenly Rose Lynne jumped up, threw the ring across the floor, and took a deep breath: "It's not real. The stupid nigger didn't even get me real jewelry. Where in the fuckin' hell am I supposed to wear shit like that?" I looked at Liliane who lowered her eyes slowly like I shouldn't say nothin'. Rose Lynne started jumpin' up and down screamin' some more. I figured out exactly where that ring was, picked it up: "Rose Lynne, you gotta calm yourself. This here is beautiful." Before I could go on, Liliane interrupted: "It's glass and goldplate, Bernadette. That's what's upsettin' her so." Now it was my turn to roll my eyes. I left them two alone.

I put the ring in my pocket, shit, found Roy was hugged up on some yellah girl with a high behind. This was too much for me. I thought bout tryin' to get back home, but I wasn't quite sure how and I didn't know where Danny was either. Eventually, Liliane came back to the party, gave Ronnie a stoneface for sure, went to Granville who put his arms around her, lips all over her, like she was gonna disappear. That's when I knew where Danny was cause I saw him jump the roses, head just missin' the hanging lanterns, shoutin' for the world to know: "Whatchu doin' with my girl, man?"

I couldn't tell him none of these niggahs would believe him, give him the time of day. There was calluses on his hands, a scar over by his chin, and real nappy hair on his head. Liliane tried to talk to him. Granville moved her out of the way. He, at least, was still colored. But the ladies of the house, who sat so prim and proper judging me, didn't ask Granville what he was doin' with Danny's girl. They asked was he invited and by whom. Danny was bein' held off Granville and away from Liliane by this security guard looked like a punch-drunk ex-fighter who kept grinnin'. You expected him to smile "Yes, massa" any second to the fathers of these children who appeared from nowhere. Liliane tried to talk to Danny over the ruckus, tryin' to find out what he was doin' there and all. Danny didn't betray me, didn't say I had invited him or nothin'. Then one of the ladies, the one with processed blond hair and a passel of what must be real jewelry, ordered one of the other mothers to call the police.

I know Liliane pleaded with Danny to leave peaceably. I know after she said that she went off with Granville, her head on his shoulder like she was exhausted from all this colored mess. Danny was just standin' there, surrounded by the fathers and the guard. The police came, talked police talk about trespassin'. I didn't look back once. I put that ring on my finger and went to catch the Q-44 with Danny. They didn't want the ring cause it wasn't real enough. They didn't want us cause we was too real. Our feelings was really hurt, you know. Liliane always stood up for us when her papa was round, or her mama. Liliane'd never made fun of a soul we knew or looked down on anybody we knew. The night was sickening still, foreign like Granville's accent. The bus was takin' a long time. Cars slowed when they passed like those folks could decide from lookin' if we should even be on the corner. I'd started to cry a little, but Danny kicked a trash can, leapt up on a tree limb hangin' by our heads, singin':

*I'm sendin' out an S.O.S. because I'm in so much distress*
*And if you see my baby if anybody sees my baby*
*Stop her on sight*

*Hey hey hey I'm sendin' an S.O.S.*
*Hey hey hey I'm sendin' an S.O.S.*

—EDWIN STARR

# Room in the Dark VIII

——— Well, I guess I finally started to straighten some of this mess out.

——— I didn't know things were crooked.

——— Awright, let's lighten up on the "cute" factor, here. Okay?

——— It's your session, Liliane. But "cute" or "ugly" is of little significance.

——— See. You just don't know how to leave things alone.

——— What would you have me leave alone?

——— This is hard enough as it is, without having to mull over my every single word and pause. I'll forget what I wanted to say and where I was going with it.

——— So now you are composing your sessions before you even see me?

——— No, this is what I'm talking about. You're confusing me.

——— What seems confusing may in fact be the beginning of understanding.

——— Jesus. All I wanted to tell you was that I called Daddy.

——— Yes.

——— I called Daddy. I asked him right out where my mother was.

——— Yes.

——— I said "Daddy, I know Mommy didn't die. Where did she go? And how could you do this to me? How could you?"

——— That was very brave, Liliane.

——— You're as crazy as he is. How can it be brave to live with the truth, when the lie was so much worse.

——— Not everyone is able to do that.

——— Not able to do what?

——— Not everyone is able to see the heinous in "lies" that support what is their truth, or truths. It's easier sometimes to imagine that lies are true, so we can avoid having to question ourselves, what our truths are.

——— His beliefs or truths are the last goddamn things on my mind. How could a grown man just change my whole life, leave me feeling like an orphan, telling people for years that my mama was dead, I didn't have a mama, when he knew the whole time that she was no more dead than me or you? Every time

I think about this my breathing is so heavy. I can't get enough air. I can't move. I feel all this pressure on my chest and my legs like I was deep-sea diving, but I haven't gone anywhere. I haven't gone anywhere at all.

——— Are you so sure, Liliane?

——— Am I so sure what? That I haven't gone anywhere? Yes. I'm right here where I always am.

——— But where you are is very different now than it was before our last time together. Your mother isn't dead. Your father lied to you for so many years that the truth is now suspect and tenuous. You are not a little girl whose mother is at the bottom of the sea somewhere.

——— Stop it. Stop it. I can't take this. I don't understand what's happened to me. I lose my best friend. My mother's not dead. I mean. I don't have a mother, don't know where in the hell she is, if she's not dead now, and all that bastard could tell me was he thought he did the best thing at the time. "I did what I thought was best at the time, my dear," like this is some reasonable response to why did you tell me my mama was dead when I know you sent her away. What could she have done that was so terrible? Who gave you the right to take my mama from me? He did what he thought best. Jesus, every time I look around white folks are fuckin' with me. No matter what I do or how I feel, I've gotta deal with these goddamn white people.

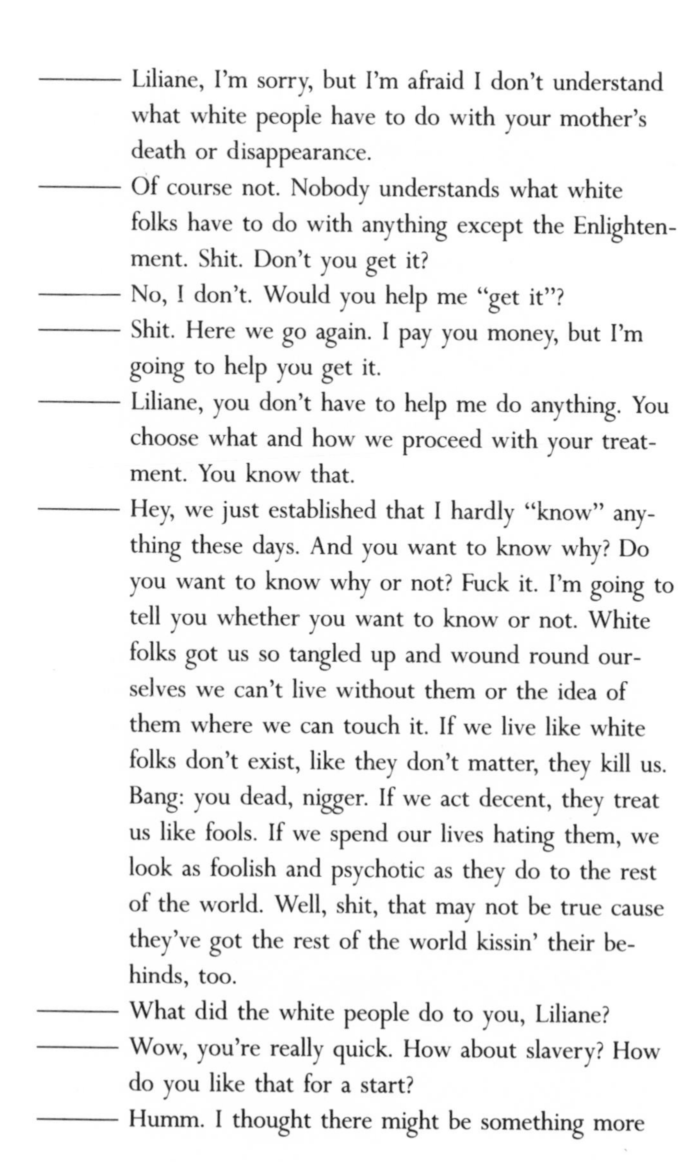

——— Liliane, I'm sorry, but I'm afraid I don't understand what white people have to do with your mother's death or disappearance.

——— Of course not. Nobody understands what white folks have to do with anything except the Enlightenment. Shit. Don't you get it?

——— No, I don't. Would you help me "get it"?

——— Shit. Here we go again. I pay you money, but I'm going to help you get it.

——— Liliane, you don't have to help me do anything. You choose what and how we proceed with your treatment. You know that.

——— Hey, we just established that I hardly "know" anything these days. And you want to know why? Do you want to know why or not? Fuck it. I'm going to tell you whether you want to know or not. White folks got us so tangled up and wound round ourselves we can't live without them or the idea of them where we can touch it. If we live like white folks don't exist, like they don't matter, they kill us. Bang: you dead, nigger. If we act decent, they treat us like fools. If we spend our lives hating them, we look as foolish and psychotic as they do to the rest of the world. Well, shit, that may not be true cause they've got the rest of the world kissin' their behinds, too.

——— What did the white people do to you, Liliane?

——— Wow, you're really quick. How about slavery? How do you like that for a start?

——— Humm. I thought there might be something more

current weighing on your mind, but perhaps I was wrong.

——— Oh, I can move it right on up to date for you, sir. What you think about us being defined as chattel or being valuable or valueless in relation to white folks? That's not too far off from slavery, is it? A white man owns you or he doesn't. We are free or slave, right? Seems pretty clear to me. Easy, even a child could understand.

——— Lili . . . here's some tissue. . . . Maybe you're crying because as a child, you didn't understand what you see as so easy, so simple.

——— I just never thought . . . It never crossed my mind that Mama'd run off with a white man.

——— Is this something your father told you?

——— Said: "Once she told me she'd always love him, I had no choice. I told her, Liliane, I told her, she'd lose you and everything we'd worked for. I couldn't let you go with her, don't you see? Darling Liliane." I don't want to talk about this anymore.

——— Liliane, you don't have to talk.

——— But, if I don't talk, how can I get better, or anything? How can I be doing my therapy, if I don't talk to you?

——— Sometimes our work is talking. Sometimes our work is simply being, experiencing feelings and thoughts we've put so far away we have no words for them. Then, the silence and our breathing allow these feelings to find the shapes and sounds of the words we need.

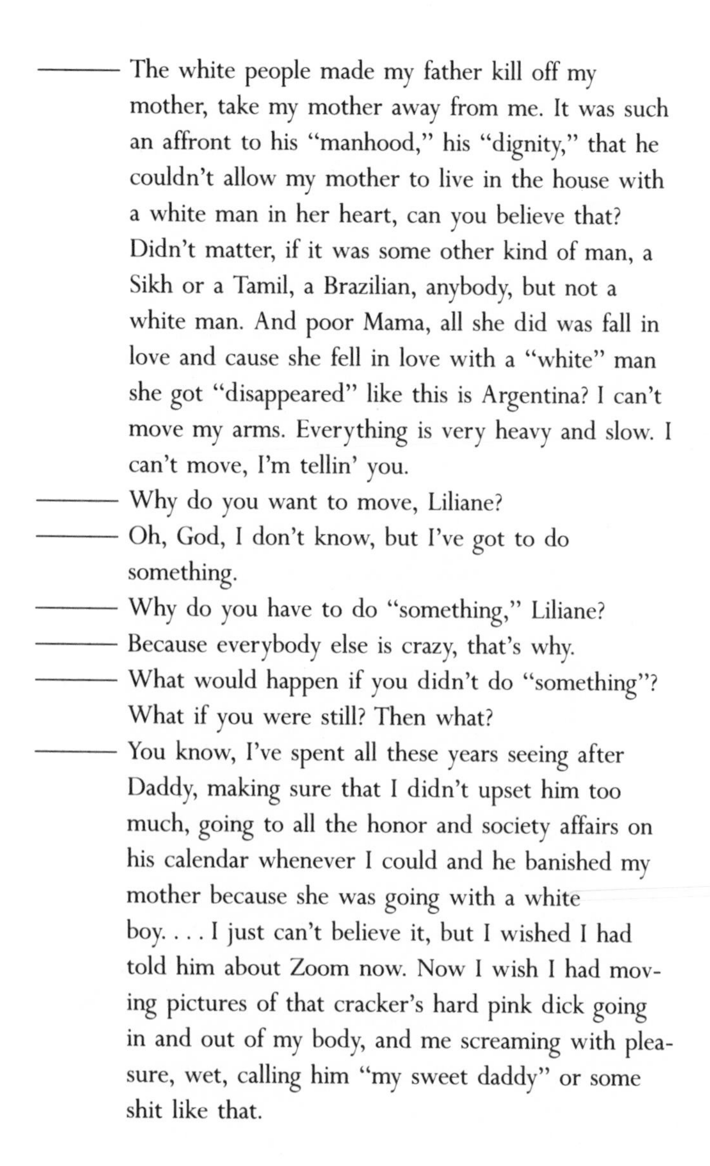

——— The white people made my father kill off my mother, take my mother away from me. It was such an affront to his "manhood," his "dignity," that he couldn't allow my mother to live in the house with a white man in her heart, can you believe that? Didn't matter, if it was some other kind of man, a Sikh or a Tamil, a Brazilian, anybody, but not a white man. And poor Mama, all she did was fall in love and cause she fell in love with a "white" man she got "disappeared" like this is Argentina? I can't move my arms. Everything is very heavy and slow. I can't move, I'm tellin' you.

——— Why do you want to move, Liliane?

——— Oh, God, I don't know, but I've got to do something.

——— Why do you have to do "something," Liliane?

——— Because everybody else is crazy, that's why.

——— What would happen if you didn't do "something"? What if you were still? Then what?

——— You know, I've spent all these years seeing after Daddy, making sure that I didn't upset him too much, going to all the honor and society affairs on his calendar whenever I could and he banished my mother because she was going with a white boy. . . . I just can't believe it, but I wished I had told him about Zoom now. Now I wish I had moving pictures of that cracker's hard pink dick going in and out of my body, and me screaming with pleasure, wet, calling him "my sweet daddy" or some shit like that.

——— Then, what would you do?
——— Then, I'd watch him have a heart attack and die. He'd turn red in the face, be so mad his jaws'd quiver. Then his eyes would get that look like a laser beam designed by colored people so it cuts quick. I'd start laughing and he'd die right in front of me. Just like that.
——— And then.
——— Then I'd be the girl who shafted her father to death on purpose and whose mother ran off with a white boy, leaving her family and the race to fend for themselves.
——— Is that what happened, Liliane?
——— No, shit. Can't you see, I don't know what happened. I mean, I know what happened to me, but none of it makes any sense to me, I mean. Daddy's always been just like he is: if I knew not to bring a white boy home, surely Mama knew it. And Daddy knew my mother was not likely to feel fulfilled in the throes of club meetings, auxiliaries, and narrow ideologies. What in the fuck were they doing together in the first place. Just doesn't add up. Well, shit, it added up to make me, didn't it?
——— Yes.
——— Maybe, you're right. . . . You know about clearing things up. Now, I understand why Daddy thought he had to watch me so carefully, intimidate boys I knew. He thought I was like my mother, and I'd run off on him. Isn't that funny?
——— Why is it funny?

——— I had no intentions or thoughts about ever leaving Daddy's house until I realized I really had to.
——— Why was that?
——— You know, doctor, kinship taboos.
——— Oh really?
——— Yeah.
——— Tell me some more about this.
——— What's to tell; a girl can't marry her father.
——— But you were just going to "kill off" your father. Nothing very romantic there.
——— No, but it might just be the kind of affection he understands.
——— Uh. Liliane, looks like we're at that time.
——— Huh, shit. I really don't want to leave right now.
——— Just remember, you don't have to do anything, just be and feel.
——— If I feel any more things, I'll lose my mind.
——— Worse things could happen.
——— I know. At least I know that.

# "Happy, Happy Birthday, Baby"
# or
# Wouldn't It Be Great
# If the Lead Singer
# of The Crests
# Wasn't a White Boy
# and I Could Be My Mother?

I do love her, but she a simple bitch, damn. You gotta flow with me here, cause I don't know any other way to explain what happened. I just got to say it like we are who we are. That's all. And wasn't nobody expectin' us to be hot 'n bothered or smart or beyond the lowest IQ in the Western Hemisphere. But it don't matter none. We're here and if all I could say is that Liliane's mother grows orchids, then shit, that's all I gotta say.

I listen to Lili. I have no choice. She's my blood. What happened to her, could just as easily be my comeuppance. I just wish she'd get out her bed and talk to me like I had some sense.

"Lollie, Lollie, listen! That's my mama wanderin' her gardens, singin'. Just a-singin' her heart out. Oh, I need to get my notebooks. Hand me that blue one. Right. And a #1 pencil.

Soft and black. Just like my mama. Lollie, stop laughin' at me. It's not my fault if I know the sun's up cause my mama is singin'. Just give me my notebook, dammit."

The sounds of their voices, fingers, and breath brushing against paper left me alone unexpectedly. These were their rituals and visions and even though I was truly "present," I was not allowed. I'd never been allowed and this never bothered me. I'm not no chump, some silly bitch who can't take herself home alone. No, sirree.

I cannot explain all this. Yet I can say I saw, I mean, I see, anything a body could see, if you wanted, I mean. These Northerners.

"Oh, Lollie."

My cousin Lili whips me cross my head. Right now. You understand? I stepped back and looked at her like if you ever do that again, I will kill you. Give it to me or if you ain't got it, get out my way. It is so easy to make these folks leap through what I know to be right now, right this moment, I thought to myself.

I have always been a hoodlum. There is nobody nowhere who could say otherwise. Plus I've always looked just like this. . . . A niggah gal with genes, good features and timing. Fuck you! I got what anybody in the world might need, whenever. And caint anybody anywhere bring alla that to you. You gotta understand. I know you understand. So, don't you fret none.

Uncle Parnell come stalkin' the hallways lookin' for some long misplaced cravat. Winona clatters in the kitchen to a breakfast gospel of grits and red-eye gravy, just for me and Mama.

"Uhm, Winona, don't you just know how to call me from

my dreams," my mama cooed, wrappin' Winona in her muscled yellah arms.

Yet Liliane and her mama were, how you call it, "nonplussed" by my mama, Aurelia, makin' herself at home. Liliane and S. Bliss exchanged flowers at the breakfast table. Lili handed her mother drawings of the blossoms Bliss groomed. And then Bliss laid a flower in Lili's palm. I ain't lyin'. When their eyes met, Bliss giggled like a precocious child, raised her left eyebrow a bit, hugged Lili, and turned jauntily to Parnell, saying: "What a delight to the eye you are this mornin', my sweet darlin'." From behind some foreign newspaper, Parnell'd grunt: "That's enough of that now, Bliss. All you sit down and eat." And then, without trying to hide at all he blushed and startin' eatin' those funny-lookin' grits with milk and sugar next to corned beef hash and eggs. See, I know for a fact can't nobody pick their family. I think even Uncle Parnell knew it. When he raised his spoon to his mouth, full with sugary grits, the man blushed. In a room fulla women he blushed cause wasn't no way he could be "not" related to us; no matter how he was intendin' to eat his grits, with sugar or without!

Winona's singin' "Caint Nobody Do Me Like Jesus," wiskin' dishes off the table, callin' all kind of mischievous spirits. To avoid the emptiness Bliss left the room with promises to return. She imagined Parnell peopled her kitchen table with his paramours and sluts, who never opened their mouths, but caroused in their silent laughter. Liliane began drawing some unknown climbin' flowerin' vine on the kitchen walls. I turned to my mama, who stepped on my toe and shushed me. Uncle Parnell smoothed his mustache, slowly risin' from his seat, biddin' his daughter "Good day." Lili's eyes followed the contours of yellow and coral roses as she drew them. When she looked at her father I bet she saw *Magnolia stellata* and Silver Jubilee roses caressing her daddy's cheeks. That's how she painted him, surrounded by flowers. To my mind, she was set on designin' a world for the three of them, a whole world just for Parnell, Bliss, and Lili herself. A world where nothin' ever became ugly or mishappen, her very best to draw her way out of what you and I gotta deal with on a day-to-day basis. Shit.

"Bye, Daddy, I'll wait up for you, okay?" Liliane chirped.

"You don't have to, darlin'," Uncle Parnell apologized.

I can hear Mama mumblin'. "Now, he don't mean one word of that, honey."

"Liliane, sweetheart, can you believe what good time Auntie Aurelia and Lollie made from St. Louis?" S. Bliss was gleamin'. She was radiant. Now, my mama was a stockier woman than S. Bliss, but not a whole lot more. She was as comfortable with her body as any unannounced Negro leftist, but more so just because we were LaFontaines and could do as we chose. We always chose ourselves or the race, which presents few dilemmas to my mind. Aurelia was buoyant as a woman's smile when a man's made love terribly well and wants more, even though she was simply sittin' in a kitchen chair, sippin' coffee.

I like to think I'm just like her: what every mother of a son warned against and every, well most, daughter's mother half prayed for, half prayed against. How did Lili put it? Bloodlines versus upward mobility; joie de vivre versus noblesse oblige. This, the nexus of post-Reconstruction alliances. Eventually, E. Franklin Frazier would come to our rescue, but at this point in time he didn't grow orchids.

"Aw, don't tell me. This our Liliane. Why I would never have believed it, if I wasn't lookin' at her myself. Bliss, you could have spit her out, I do declare!" Mama bent over Liliane's frame, wrappin' her up in a rollin' hug. Lili looked startled, looked like her eyes and body were askin' me: "Why is Aurelia doin' this to me?" I shrugged my shoulders and winked at her. What else could I do? My mama liked to getta hold of things she loved; Bliss liked to look. That's all there was to it. But Lili and I had the best of both sisters: one could hug us and one gazed.

Maybe that's why it felt so still and alone in Liliane's house. I'm used to seein' my friends, my mama's friends, and all of those folks' friends roamin' the halls of our house, almost settin' up house in our house. Everybody assumed cause S. Bliss is a LaFontaine and they are close to God that God must be very quiet.

Liliane'd been raised among her mother's orchids as if she were one herself. Where in the mix of rice and collards I know to be my life was she to surface? And then how would we survive: did anyone care?

It's time to see S. Bliss's gardens.

"Oh, good lord, Bliss, you've changed it again," my mama squealed. Her eyes widened as she swept by the arcs of paths nestled between the water lilies and weepin' willows. S. Bliss found her way to shadows where she disappeared and all my mama could see was the breadth of the garden.

With her voice floatin' like a fragrance, S. Bliss quipped: "Aurelia, I don't want my Liliane to draw the same gardens forever, you know."

Now my mama, lookin' for Bliss, lookin' like she's playin' hide 'n seek, stammers: "But, Bliss, these trees take twenty years to get this big."

As if appearin' from outta nowhere, Bliss sighs: "Yeah, I know that."

At this point, I could tell my mama didn't know who she was talkin' to: Bliss or her imagination. All this carryin' on bout some damn plants was crazy as all get out to us. Now, all of a sudden delphiniums and roses and lilies lined what would have been boxed flowerbeds were they not obscured by the luxuriance of Auntie Bliss's selections. "This is all designed for Liliane. I've a purpose here, Aurelia. Lili can come here for the rest of her life and know herself to be one of the most ravishing creatures on earth."

With some difficulty, Mama worked at a part of her dress that had snagged on a rose bush. She was just a-shakin' her head. I imagine she was makin' those sounds she makes when she's puzzled. Mama'd told me before she believed her sister Bliss'd read too many tarot cards.

I'm thinkin', thank God, those two are movin' too fast. If they ever do getta notion that I'm diggin' out here for my marijuana plants Lili promised to cultivate, it'd be my ass. That's what.

"Bliss, now you know I love you like nobody else in the world, but you can't build all this for no child, especially not a Negro child in this day and age. Why she can't even drink water some places. Plus, hear me now, if she carries on like you, she'll be dead before either one of us: me or you. How's that sit with your fancy ways and dreamin's?"

Auntie Sunday, I like callin' her that, brought the petal of some flower (you know I don't know what they callt), well, she brought the petal of some flower to her lips and cheek so delicately. I thought she might actually pass out, you know, swoon, from the touch of it, but that's too much for me to fathom. A flower petal's gointa run off with all my senses. Yet, Sunday seemed none the worse for wear, if you get what I mean. She turned to my mama like she just been blessed by the Pope himself:

"Aurelia, she won't have to be anything at all like you or me. She won't have to construct herself a garden of love; a garden of early delights, so to speak. Ha. She'll have the whole real world. She and Lollie, they'll have the whole world to make their own, their home."

"Lollie does not need no garden of love. I'm tryin' my best to keep her truck-farmin', and you should do the same." My mama was doin' her very best to keep from stompin' on Bliss's flowers, leaves and all. S. Bliss moved very slowly like women do when they are about to do the tango:

"Aurelia, I am not always going to be here. I'm not always going to be married to Parnell, either." Then, she stood so tall with her chest opened like a classical dancer taught right. She looked round the garden, all them damned flowers and funny-shaped leaves, and she continued: "I have never been what anybody expected, or wanted for that matter: I'm not even what I wanted."

My mama doesn't care where she is right now. She cocks her head, hand on her hip:

"Sunday Bliss LaFontaine, have you lost your mind? 'Not

what you wanted.' Your whole life's not about anythin' but what you want! Don't put on with me. I've known you all your life!"

Mama was tryin' to keep track of what she was sayin', she was so beside herself, but I noticed somethin' that tripped me right out. I realized as they walked along that square sections of Bliss's garden gave way to diagonals that kept pace with the slope of the land, and ended up in the shape of a cross. I'm tellin' you no lie. S. Bliss, that bitch, designed a Eden that turned into her crucifixion. And my mama's walkin' around in it with her. Ain't that nothin'?

When they finally got to the gazebo, at least I was relieved. Aurelia didn't have enough sense to tend to her ownself. She's up there askin' Auntie Bliss questions bout her private life:

"Well, Bliss, are you sure there's nothin' you want to tell me? There is nothin' the family hasn't heard before, believe you me. You know I mean it. You can tell me anythin'." Then, my mama, she laid back on the latticework of the peach-toned gazebo like she'd done all she had to do. And Auntie Bliss, she's waltzin' around like she still has one of those flowers in her mouth:

"Parnell is Parnell. That's a constant factor. But Parnell isn't nearly as progressive as you'd like to believe he is."

"Bliss, I don't want to believe nothin' about your Parnell. I just want to believe whatever you tell me."

"What I'm tellin' you, straight off. There's nothin' Parnell Lincoln's got that I want. Nothin'." I see Bliss get up in my mother's face like she got no shame at all. Bliss hisses:

"I'm sick of it. I'm sick of all of it. The posturin', and frontin', the fuckin' grandeur of it. I'm sick. I'm sick and tired of it all. Do you understand me?"

Aurelia whips S. Bliss to the seesaw with one hand. She's mad now, you hear. With Bliss gruntin' and groanin' underneath her, my mama growls: "What about Lili? Whatchu gonna do with Liliane, heifer?"

"Leave her with her father! What'd you think I was about to do?"

Then, I saw my mama turn around and slap S. Bliss, Sunday Bliss, herself, with the back of her hand with as much force as she could muster, and believe me, I know. There was a sudden quietness, a quiet made me tremble. The two of them standin' there in that gazebo like the world'd come to an end, leastways their world anyway.

"Nobody leaves a LaFontaine. Nobody leaves a LaFontaine child anywhere, not less they dead."

"Well, I'm not goin' to die just so I can live my own life. And dammit, look at her. She doesn't even look like a La-Fontaine. Look at her, dammit. I can't even imagine how's she related to me. I can't. I can't explain how she happened. I can't. I just can't."

Aurelia steps back, confused, as far as I can tell. She's shakin' her head again. That's not good, either.

"That girl thinks the world of you, bitch. She lives and breathes for you to simply spend some of your time with her. Look at her. Shit. I been watchin' you all her life, makin' the world pretty, makin' yourself pretty, so maybe she wouldn't notice whatever in the hell you think is so 'ugly' bout her. Oh, no. I don't need to look at Lili and see she's not a LaFontaine.

All I've gotta do is take one look at you and know you never have been."

Auntie Bliss starts tuggin' on my mama's clothes, talkin' about: "Don't say that, 'Relia. Please don't say that."

Mama pulls away from her real brusquelike: "I can only say what's true, Bliss. Only what's true. Now I know, your truth and mine got nothin' in common. Nothin' at all." Then my mama walked backward from her sister Bliss, shakin' her head again, mumblin' again. Sunday Bliss lay crouched on the floor of the gazebo, cursin' Parnell, Lili, and the LaFontaine family in general. She went on and on til finally I thought to myself, couldn't be nobody else left for her to put the evil eye or 666 or a Klan cross or nothin' on. There wasn't nobody left for her tongue to whip, for the gods she worshipped to come after.

"Dear Holy Mother, I really want my mommy to understand that I don't know everything that she knows, but I am devoting my life to all that she is and believes. Please, forgive me." Then, Lili fell to her knees and began to genuflect before all the Virgin Mothers from *Nossa Senhora do Rosario* to *La Virgen de Guadalupe*. "The breath between what I might be and what I want so much is as real as the blood of your Son, *Nuestro Senhor,* flowing down his arms. Please, I beg of you, help me, now."

Even though I know what I know and I saw what I saw, be it Liliane or her mother, I'm standin' there in Lili's doorway half believin' she was right. There's no way in hell a LaFontaine woman left a room lookin' like this. Here we got clothes, shoes, candies, books, paints, pencils, sweaters, and all kinds of papers every which way. So I say:

"Lili, you need to pray for somebody to clean this mess up, that's what you need to do!" I had to clear myself a path so I could reach her behind.

"What are we gonna do now?" I'm askin' cause I want to get out of Lili's mess, Sunday Bliss's mess and the mess Aurelia was bout to make of me if I let Lili know any of this mess was goin' on at all.

"Well, I'm going to finish these portraits of my mommy. Then I've got some drawings of her new orchids to do before the light changes too dramatically." Liliane somehow positioned herself on the bed so she could hold a pencil, look out the window, and draw as well as talk to me.

"I'm thinkin' bout investigatin' the whereabouts of those young boys in town you always talkin' bout. That's what I'm thinkin'." Here I am lookin' in the mirror at myself more than good, I must say. Then I turn around to look at Lili. She's still sittin' up there drawin' some more pictures of her mama, Sunday Bliss LaFontaine-Lincoln. "Lili Lincoln," I said and she didn't turn around. "Liliane LaFontaine-Lincoln, don't you have enough pictures of your mother?"

"Not really." Lili's face brightened at my mention of the woman she thought truly the most beautiful woman in the world. "Besides, we have to wait for Mommy and Aunt Aurelia to go play cards. Then, we have to wait for Papa to go wherever it is he goes."

I'm thinkin' to myself, are any of these people in this same house or garden or ravine, whatever this is, at the same time? Do they know each other at all?

Liliane didn't say anythin' for awhile. When she spoke, she didn't take her pencil off the paper. Lili kept her focus. She was drawin' a poppy, a single scarlet poppy by her mother's cheek.

"Mommy says there's very little worthwhile in life, if we can't see it. She says we see most things comin' our way, but we blind ourselves to it. That's why I draw everything. I want to see what's up, what's coming my way."

I am too through with all this damn talk. "I awready told you: What I want to come my way is one of Danny's lil cousins you always talkin' bout. . . . That's what I want. Do you understand me?"

Lili looked up from her notebook, a bit distracted: "If you want a niggah that bad, draw one."

I know when somebody's gettin' fixed to fight with me, so I threw a piece of charcoal at her:

"I don't want no niggah on paper. Shit." I was so mad I could feel my platinum hair clingin' to my forehead and my cheeks flushin' like I was Sally Starr on some unruly horse.

"If you use your imagination, Lollie, they don't stay confined to a two-dimensional plane." Lili is finishin' the stem of this poppy by her mother's cheek: rockin' and drawin', rockin' and drawin' til a big grin burst off her face: "See, Lollie, I told you. If you want it, draw it."

I'm bout fit to be tied. "If I gotta do all that, I don't want no niggah. . . . I want that white boy who's the lead singer with The Crests. He's so fine. Good God. He likes niggahs, too."

"Lollie, I must say that's white of him." Lili responded slowly, never interrupting her strokes.

"You said to draw whatever I wanted," I spat back.

"Yeah. Well, I didn't think I had to say it."

"Say what? What are you talkin' about?"

That's me talkin', bouncing up and down on the bed, tryin' to break her concentration.

"We don't draw white men in this house. Johnnie Maestro or any other cracker, not here. Is that clear?"

"You said use my imagination," I told her right back.

"Then, imagine something else, heifer." Liliane dismissed my early mornin' fantasies and turned again to her work: her flowers, her mother's face among the flowers and her dreams. All of a sudden she leapt up from her drawing papers with this strange grin, light in her eyes: "If anyone in this house ever brings home a white boy, then Johnnie Maestro is not white and my papa's dead."

Liliane thought this was funny. I wasn't gonna be the one to tell her "The Twistin' Postman" had a letter in his hands and it wasn't good news. It's just that I'd never known a black man wanted a woman who didn't want her children. And that means to me, I know I'm not all that grown, but if a Negro man's not sniffin' after her mother, that only leaves a white man knockin' at the door. And that means, accordin' to Liliane, herself, there won't be nobody home. Damn. Lili can't even sing The Shirelles' song:

*Mama said there'd be days like this*
*There'd be days like this*
*My mama said, Mama said, Mama said.*

—THE SHIRELLES

Lili in all her colors and flowers. She can't even sing this simple, beautiful little bitty ol' song.

# Room in the Dark IX

——— Well, hello, there. . . .

——— Hello, Liliane. How are you?

——— I was singing to you again, just like in the beginning.

——— Really? What were you singing?

——— Some old black magic.

——— That's pretty potent stuff as far as I know.

——— I can testify to that.

——— So, now, we are our own church?

——— Let's not get carried way here.

——— But doesn't making witness open conduits to the gods, and with the puissance of the deities available aren't we capable of speaking in tongues, eating fire, shape-shifting, et cetera?

——— I'd say something flippant, but I did change shape

last night and I did speak, a particularly peculiar . . . I don't know what to call it, how do you say whatever climbing plants talk.

——— What does that sound like, Lili?

——— I'm not actually sure I can tell you, but I was a labyrinthine rhododendron last night.

———

——— I thought I must have looked at too much Frida Kahlo.

——— That's plausible, I can imagine.

——— I thought I was imagining it, but I was sitting in my window, the one that faces the avenue, watching the car lights, the people coming and going any places I determined, when I realized that the vines of the rhododendron I was sitting under had grown into my braids. At first this didn't bother me much, but then I remembered I had artichokes on the stove, but I couldn't move because I'd become this plant. I really got angry cause this was my plant that I'd nurtured and fed, turned toward sunlight and away, washed the leaves, soaked in the tub, led along silk strings to the ceiling. Who was going to feed me? That's what I wanted to know.

——— That's a very "Lili" fantasy.

——— How's that?

——— There's all the glass in the window. You are watching lights and people moving about.

——— So?

——— Didn't your mother have a greenhouse?

——— Yes.

——— Didn't she nurture rare flowers in the greenhouse? And entertain a variety of people whose identities you imagined.

——— Yes.

——— And you wondered about what kinds of things, Liliane, when your mother was tending to her friends?

——— Who was going to feed me.

——— And take care of you, wash you, dry off your limbs, lead you toward the sun, and then, higher, toward the ceilings, the heights of a self that is you, Liliane.

——— All that was in there?

——— Yep.

——— Don't "yep" me. Tell me who's gonna feed me.

——— Didn't you say you were cooking some artichokes?

——— Yes.

——— What else were you cooking?

——— Oh, how would I know. No, don't tell me, "It's your dream, Lili."

——— You're right about that.

——— I know I'd made a salad awready. My table was set, I had salmon in white sauce and capellini.

——— Seems like a balanced, nutritious meal. . . .

——— But I couldn't get up to get to the kitchen.

——— Why was that?

——— Because I was a rhododendron.

——— That had very long vines. . . .

——— Oh, yes, they went all the way to the ceiling and back to the floor. . . . I see what you mean.

——— Hummmn.

——— I didn't see how far I could go. If I had, I'd have

been able to go anywhere in my house that I cared to. . . .

——— Or had to.

——— It's funny, Jesus.

——— What's funny?

——— The last lines to that song I was singing to you: "Ain't it funny how time slips away." And I could say I almost "let my vines slip away."

——— Polished, healthy, strong vines at that.

——— Oh, by the way, Brook Benton sang that song.

——— So, Lili. Here's some trivia for you. Who sang the song, forgive me if the melody's a bit off, "I'm giving you your freedom. . . ."

——— Say what, we're finished? Done? Kaput? [She sings.] "Just like that?"

——— No, no. Not quite "Just like that." But soon.

——— Oh, okay. Cause I've got a lot more songs I want to sing.

——— And paintings, I hope.

——— Paintings, drawings, funny little wood-shaped things, sand castles, watercolors, #2 pencil sketches, and . . .

——— And?

——— The rest of me, but that really won't happen. "Just like that." [She sings.]

——— No, that won't happen. "Just like that." [They sing and Liliane keeps singing.] And now, it really is time.

——— You are, as The Drifters say, "Some kinda wonderful."

——— You are, too, Lili. You are, too.

# Every Time My Lil World Seems Blue, I Just Haveta Look at You and Learn Eye-Hand Coordination

Eye-hand coordination is what takes so long. Just look, not watch, the figure. Let my hand move along the same lines as my eyes. Let my hand go where my eyes go. At this rate I may be finished drawing this young man, maybe, next year, when twin full moons hang outside my window. This is not the most ethical of experiments. I don't have any idea who this young man is. I am indulging in anonymous sexual stimulation. Does that make me as venal as that stoop-shouldered Greek deli-delivery man I stood behind at the Rite-Aid counter? His face couldn't have been more than two inches away from some sleek girlie magazine centerfold. Made me wonder, if this was one of those scratch-and-smell bonuses I'd heard about at an antiporn meeting not too long ago. So, here's this grown man with his face up inside this centerfold. From where I was standing, all that was visible were two ankle-height boots with very very high, come-fuck-me heels fitting into both of his hands, like in the circus when acrobats balance flying women in their hands. Then, two equally parallel legs creep from his rather stubby fingers to his forehead, so he looks to me like a fellow growing tawny calves and suede boots from his skull.

He must have felt my eye disclaiming his behavior as the activity of a healthy adult. He dropped the magazine, featuring the legs that belonged, it turns out, to a smiling white woman holding her backside open where the staple was. He jumped back, looked up at me, smiled. With aplomb, I said, "Sir, you've dropped your magazine." He replies, "Oh?" I point directly to the stapled anus, "There." Blushing, the deli man brushes his hand across his mouth, mumbles, "I'm finished."

Eye-hand coordination. Eye-hand coordination, that's what makes a certain kind of painter. This guy is definitely not going to be a painter. He's still looking at his magazine, now.

There's this place, a spot, on the mid-West Side where I used to meet a fella who stayed with me off and on. Well, I used to see him. I stopped going out with him because he had this terrible habit of wearing my shirts to meet me. Now I am virtually sure he wasn't a cross-dresser or something, someone who just adores putting on women's clothes. I think he was one of those men who was working on himself, you know. The man of his times not afraid of his female side, his softness and all that. I'm not against any of that, but I'm not sure that men's consciousness-raising groups in the forest with animal skins and drums is the path to their female side. Plus, I resented him, his name was Alex, for that matter. I can find no good reason for him to constantly show up in my clothes. It's amusing before making love, I guess; to exchange things, roles, scents. Yet I can't help thinking that he's actually not investing his own money, the time it takes to find these particular garments, that . . . Well, they look like me.

Maybe Alex imagined wrapping me around and about him when he slipped those wiry arms in my sleeves. The wildest thing I can conjure up is that when he put my pants on that was some simulation of fucking. I don't know. I just got aggravated when he'd casually appear with none of my hips or bust and look perfectly adorable. Alex could probably have walked all over Manhattan naked if it wasn't against the law, and come to meet me, too. Oh, whatta husky cherub he was: eyes so deep I could wake all up in them; lanky, wiry brown taut like wound hemp. Maybe he wasn't such a bad idea after all. He could've worn my shirts so he'd be closer to me. Now, that could be interesting, a fellow with a fetish for me. Maybe Alex didn't actually have anything to wear, hummh.

Anyway I met him at this place that had one of the deepest juke boxes, had the greatest B.B. King, The Orlons, The Cadillacs, even The Five Satins. For fifty cents I could enter any rollicking summer of my life, any New Year's Eve, every teenaged dream and take Alex with me. I probably was too hard on him, expecting familiarity with a past I didn't share or refer to, unless some ditty by Ruby and the Romantics or Mary Wells grabbed me up.

I can't exactly say what Alex did with a lot of the time he had on his hands. He was gone a lot, on the road a lot with this rock band or that avant-garde group. He wasn't a musician, I was boycotting musicians at that time, but I didn't quite find my way out of "the industry," you know what I mean? So, Alex did lights, sound, road management, that sort of thing. Thank goodness I am not a groupie. Never was. But I don't feel in charge of what I'm doing now. I am not able to move this pencil off my paper, nice heavy-grained paper I searched for yesterday, knowing I would come here today to draw this man I don't know and then take all that I drew from and of him home with me again.

What baffles me is that this is the same table I would sit at to wait for Alex, always-in-my wardrobe Alex, yet there's none of him around me. All I manage to do day after day is to go look at art: Julian Schnabel, Brice Marden, Jennifer Bartlett, "The Nigger Drawings," and I end up here looking for him. How, you say, can I obsessively seek out a man of whom I have no knowledge? I know the nape of his neck from ten feet, how his braids fall over his shoulder blades, the angle of his chin when he laughs, the curve of the delts and the arrogance of his posture, his ease among friends. I just look at him. I watch and my hands do the rest. I keep coming back on some ritual of expiation. I've burned no candles, strewn no flowers, asked no questions. And this is a place to ask some questions. Lemme tell ya, if there's some dirt to be had, dug up or fabricated, we are in heaven. From the bathroom to the bar is a nest of intrigue, seductive badinage, and income-appropriate drug trade. Remarkable insights offered from all quarters. That's not including the Men's Room. I have some friends, rather acquaintances, who pass through. Nadia who must be one of the most beautiful women in the world: deep copper like wildflower honey, a laugh like a million snuggles, the libido of a Great Dane in heat. She was a professional back-up singer, Frankle Calle, Lou Rawls, John Cougar Mellencamp. She had all the looks, the voice, and the coke. A couple of high-living Guadaloupeans gave the place a twinge of sophistication. Otherwise, it was straight-up industry profilin' or procurin' of pussy, or cocaine, whatever made you happy. Name that tune, baby.

It's not that no one paid me no mind. I sent any number of evil "don't sit your ass down here" looks at men who were gracious, good-looking, well nourished, I always pay attention to that. All I wanted was to draw this man with the braids who sat just beyond an arch that separated the serious diners from the middling drug-booty cruisin' set. He always had a full meal. I found something exciting in that. What he wanted to eat. The muscles he used when he raised his fork to his mouth and set it down, how he pulled brown bread with raisins apart and spread real butter. I am telling you this from inference. I can't see his face. Never tried to. What would be the point? I come every day. I sit right here and wait. He comes every day and sits right there. I draw as much of him as his time allows, before he's surrounded by these women who've made an art of themselves. When the curls and busts start to hover, I pick up my things and take the local train home. That way it takes longer to leave him. I don't like wanting anything too much, that's just my way. In a fit of independence one evening, I think Little Willie John was singing something, I bounced off to the ladies' room with my friend, Nadia. We must have stood outside those two itsy-bitsy stalls all of a half hour before these girls couldn't anybody hardly see if it wasn't for ALL them eyelashes and bags coming ahead of them, came falling right down in front of us. We could have laughed, I guess, but we were getting ready to powder our noses, too. I swear I've spent as much care and energy examining Nadia's nose for traces of white powder as I spent seeing to myself. I had lived with a junkie once who was adamant that being a junkie didn't mean one had to look like a junkie straight off.

Well, Nadia and I got right lit up. I forgot about my other obsession. I even told Nadia, there was a guy right outside who'd give Teddy Pendergrass or Reggie Jackson a run for they money outside this very door. But we didn't budge. Stayed up in that mirror like goddamned Snow White's stepmama. Oh, Jesus, talk about some *peligrosa* foolishness.

Somehow Nadia and I managed to stumble and giggle our way back to the cafe itself. She was in amazing suede shorts that made me reconsider the significance of thighs. No matter, we came screeching and hooting bout stuff that was nobody's business into the rush of the late supper crowd as opposed to the early morning crowd which was a boisterous collection of educated hoodlums. We hushed abruptly. That's how folks were looking at us like we should hush. We did.

I looked up by the arch to fine dining and he was gone. He was gone. I heard The Chantels weeping "He's gone, My baby left me." But I don't know who this guy is. Nadia thinks I made him up, he exists in my mind, she says. I'm having a panic attack. I go to my notebooks. There he is. There he is again. He's real. I've got him right here. I look up. Heads of Sly Stone–looking muthafuckahs get in my way. Jerri-Curl and Luther van Dross types block my view. *Boyz,* early in the scene, put they nasty-lookin' sweatshirt-hooded heads in my way. I don't know what he looks like. I mean, only I know what he looks like. He's disappeared. I can't breathe. I can't find him. I push the cognac Nadia's brought me aside. I decide to search for him. He could not have left. He means too much to me. He cannot be gone.

Trying to get niggahs busy chatting up a girl to get out of my way is almost a lost cause. I think their feet grow in my direction when I'm not looking for them, but somebody else. Trip bitch! their feet proclaim. I keep looking in men's faces. Other men I don't know. I don't know his face, either. I should walk backward, looking for his braids. I know his braids, black twists they are really not braids at all. They come down his back like a black surf; like black string cheese. I know this. I should go backward. He would never have left me. I take him home every night. I take him home with me.

*And I can't find him.*
*And I don't know how to ask for him.*
*I don't know his face, though I feel it.*
*I don't know his name, though I breathe it.*

I sleep under a six-foot incarnation of his braids in bronze. This is not funny. I'm not in control of this. I can't stop myself from laughing. I need to find this guy I don't know. Yeah. Everybody does, they say, "I don't know his name, but I'll recognize him." "Right!" "Baby, you sure you not talkin' bout me?" "Look close, now."

Why everybody look so seedy? Everything so stink and nasty? The place deserted, still fulla these no-count sycophants. What else to do, but find the music. Go directly to the jukebox, Liliane. Find a melody, Lili. Go get you some music. I brush by smells of bourbon, musk, weed, and sweat. Any other time I'd at least check out a silhouette, but not now. I get to the jukebox, temporary Promised Land. Thank you, Jesus. Lemme see. Lemme see. Lemme see. Yes, The Shirelles, "Blue Holiday," Barrett Strong, "I Apologize," and Willie Colon, "The Hustler." For me. I dedicate all this to myself. Nadia is rubbing up behind me like she's bout to pee on herself. "What in the hell do you want, Nadia? He disappeared. He's outta here and you, you sposed to know every goddamed thing and you don't know who I could be talkin' bout."

"Now. Hold your horses, Miz whatchamacallit. . . . All I said was I couldn't place nobody quite how you explained. Sound like Gabriel and his horn on a Concorde jet or something."

"I don't make fun of you like that," I stammered. Well, what difference did it make. I've got my drawings, got my bronze braids, and I ain't got my feelings hurt.

That's not quite true. I'd grown dependent on this set of shoulders. That's not like me, to give up so much to a man's guardianship. I'd worked with fire and peculiar mixes of metals to fashion myself a canopy in his image. I was bashful, demure even, when I pictured myself before him. And we know I don't know who he is. Well, the crux of it is that I wanted a technologically proficient Third World man to enter the twenty-first century with me. I know, I know a barbarian when I see one. I know I'll know the King of Kings, when it's that time. I know this boy ain't the Apocalypse, but you can't hear it? Oh God, whenever I see the line from his elbow to his earlobe, Carla Thomas jumps all over my ass talkin' bout, "Gee whiz." Is this the real nature of pornography? Have I lost my mind and any sense of integrity a feminist has to have to be taken seriously? There's a possibility that no one can tell. He's not like a tattoo or scarification, I mean.

Can you tell by looking?

"No."

"Nadia, shut up. He could take you to his house and bring you back in six weeks and you wouldn't know."

I'm going to down a magnum of Perrier & Jouët in my black satin teddy and the lace panties with the open crotch. I'm gonna stay home and draw drawings of the drawings of him that I've got. I'm not going to come out of my house until there are some hip black people in outer space. I'm not going to play me some Ruth Brown records, eat hominy grits with brown oyster sauce and do all the things I been told make a woman feel like a woman should.

I'm going to the telephone that's not a direct line to the coke man, so I can see if this guy who sorta likes me is busy. This is so crazy. I know I gotta do some reality work here. Call a man you know, Lili. Don't go all the way on out there, darling. Call Alex, see if he wants to wear some of your clothes, while you walk round naked. All right. Don't call Alex. Be a class A lunatic and sleep neath them metallic dreadlocks hanging over your bed. Nothing kinky there, huh? I am trying to let my tears fall in my snifter like Courvoisier got the best of me. I want to ask Nadia to take me to the ladies room again. For a quick toot or two. I want to stand. I liked what his beauty brought out of me. Eye-hand coordination and all. I'm thinking maybe the rush from the enigma he is is sufficient. That'll get me through, you know. Right on cue, some side man plays The Isley Brothers, "Love the One You're With." I feel my *survivor* kick in and take a deep breath. She lets me run my tongue over my lips. Chastises me for gritting my teeth, helps me tilt my chin with insouciance. Now, we ready? she asks.

When I raise my eyes and feel all that defiance burning behind my lashes, I'm struck dumb.

He's walking toward me.

He's smiling at me.

His braids fall over his chest too. I'd never allowed for that.

I'd never imagined seeing him face to face.

I'd never meant to ask his name.

I'm losing my breath, he's lifting off the ground.

He's whispering my name, "Liliane, Lili, Lili." I know I don't know this man. I steal up on him in the late afternoon in a studio musicians' hangout. Nobody, only Nadia knows me, here. I never said anything to him.

"Lili," he takes my mouth in his and I lose any semblance of anatomical realities. How, how, how, could such a man know me already? I am staring, an imbecile, *une idiote joyeuse*. I'm managing to smile. I can't help myself.

I am touching the rafters of my dreams when all of a sudden The Isley Brothers' sideman's selection "Shout" blares all round me in a twirling swish of me in his arms in this den of iniquity that was clearly Eden. I should think so, I said to myself, trying to steady myself from a true swoon'n' faint.

"Yeah, *sí*. Liliane."

"The artist?"

"Yeah, most of the time, yeah."

"I haven't seen you since you let all those blackbirds free out some tower you built in Port-au-Prince a couple of years ago."

"You mean, the birds with messages from the first free Africans in the New World."

"Well, baby, they weren't the first free ones . . ."

"The first ones freed by their own armed struggle."

"Right . . . I gave you a message to put on one of them. Don't you remember?"

I am feeling my face get red, so red I'm going to explode. I can't say anything. I am talking to the man I've even been taking home with me every night, a man I don't know. He says he's been in one of my projects. And how he has, every sinew, contraction, and gesture. Yes.

"Liliane, are you alright? Can I get you something?"

I still can't say anything. I just shout for a colored joy, a gritty pelvis-born glee rises up outta my throat and I haveta smile to let it out.

"Oh, pick me up and kiss me again. Then we can talk all night long."

"You sure," he says with a twinkle in his eyes would make a guy with eyes in the back of his head jealous.

"Oh yes," I say.

"You know what my message on the free-flying bird said?"

"No, of course not. They went out in the sky around the world tied up in our dreams and desires to be found like anything else that's sacred."

"My message said, now I wrote it out by hand, now, my message said, 'I want to see this woman again without machetes and barbed wire so close.' "

"C'mon, now."

"Seriously, I thought about that a lot. You sending them birds anywhere they wanted to fly with whatever wishes anybody brought you. I never thought I'd run into you again, though."

"I've been . . . Could you put here, here, your left hand by my cheek. Yeah. Humm. I've been trying to draw this."

"What?"

"This feeling, your hand from this angle, there."

"Lili, I'm not sure I'm gettin' all this. Go slower."

"No, you don't want me to go slower. I'll get too confused. Just let me tell you the truth."

"Well, okay, but everything's alright."

"No. No. Everything is not alright. I've been drawing you. Every day from right over there. Eye-hand coordination. I was working on. I practiced getting you just right. I sleep underneath braids, huge bronze braids like yours, I made from drawings of you I took home every day. And I never said hello to you or asked how you were feeling."

I'm every shade of purple now. I am crying. He lifts my chin. I do not look at him. I cannot.

"What's wrong with that? You're an artist, right?"

"Yes. I was perfecting eye-hand coordination."

"Fine. That's good."

I feel his forearm tween my waist and my ribcage, lava, a house music triple-threat bass mix.

"Yeah. Now all you gotta do is kiss me again. Then tell me your name, so, I know how to say, please do it again. . . ."

"Thayer."

"Thay . . ." I want to have a decent conversation, but his tongue is all up, back in my mouth so all I can do is remember drawing with my heart. My hands are swept up in muscles, Aretha's wail is coaxing me off my feet.

*"And I ain't never, no no. Loved a man the way that I/I love you."*

But that's me, Lili, sayin' "Kiss me once again. Thayer, don't you never, never, say that we're through, cause I ain't never loved a man the way that I've, I've drawn you."

# Room in the Dark

# X

——— You don't haveta tell me.

——— Tell you what, Lili?

——— I can't keep Sierra, that's what.

——— I have never said you can't keep Sierra.

——— I can't keep Sierra anymore than I can keep a wish or a dream. We can't hold on to dreams either, can we?

——— Lili, I am not sure I am following you. Is it Sierra you can't keep or your dreams?

——— Both. I can't keep anything. Nothing. . . . It's ridiculous.

——— Dreams are ridiculous? Sierra too?

——— Don't play a jackass, now. You know goddamn well what I mean.

——— I don't know anything you don't tell me, Lili. That's the truth.

——— Oh, go to hell.

———

——— I was Roxie's best friend. I tried to help her, before . . .

——— . . . before Tony killed her.

——— Yes. Before Tony killed her, she was my best friend. She met Tony at Hotel Nacional where I took her for a few drinks, ha! I translated for them in between sets when he could talk to her. Then, later on I helped her with her letters to him. . . .

——— But you didn't meet him when the dinghies and yachts came in from Mariel, did you?

——— No, Roxie did.

——— See, Lili, we sort of danced around this issue before. Roxie had a child with Tony, was in love with Tony, and was killed by Tony. There is nothing you could have done about any of that.

——— I know that. I know all that, but now they're gonna take Sierra from me, too. After all this, they're gonna take her. . . .

——— Why do you think you are crying so, Lili?

——— Cause they're gonna take my baby, my beautiful Sierra. They're gonna take her like nothin' happened.

——— But whose baby was wrenched from her mother's arms?

——— Roxie's.

——— Roxie's, R. C. Golightly's, and S. Bliss.

——— What has she got to do with this? Roxie never left me or betrayed me. How can you mention her name in the same breath as my best friend and her mother! Have you lost your mind?

——— No, Lili, you lost your mother.

——— So?

——— Some of this pain, a good deal of the pain you are feeling now, as you prepare Sierra to go to her grandparents, is justifiably your own. In Sierra you have "lil Lili" who can be guided by you, the adult Lili, through the dense and haunting loss the death of Roxie presents, in a way that was impossible for you as "baby" Lili. . . . Do you understand?

——— You mean I can't help her?

——— No. That's not what I'm saying. You can help her. . . . You simply have to know that that is what you are doing.

——— Wha—What about me, then? How can I help . . . me? Who are these "lil Lilies" and "baby Lilies"? I'm a big grown woman, what in the hell can I do for a "lil" me and a "baby" me?

——— A lot. There's a lot you can do.

——— Like what?

——— For one thing, we can take better care of lil Lili.

——— We could do that?

——— Yes.

——— That's really good cause I lost all the babies last night.

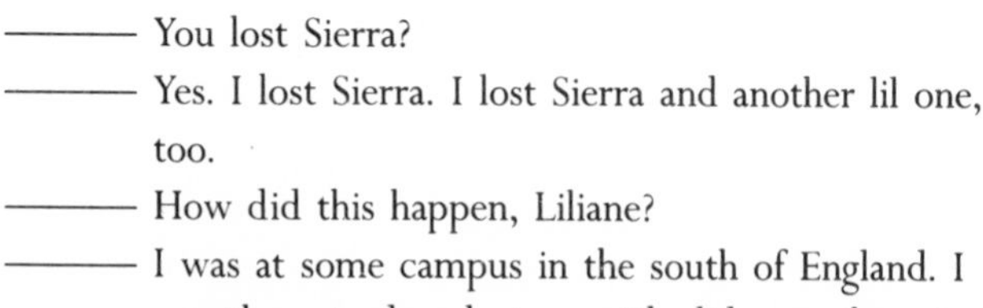

——— You lost Sierra?

——— Yes. I lost Sierra. I lost Sierra and another lil one, too.

——— How did this happen, Liliane?

——— I was at some campus in the south of England. I was there to do a lecture with slides on the art of the Americas. I started out with a monologue by Guillermo Cabrera-Infante and a slide, *A Bride for the Gods* by Wilfredo Lam. Some Argentinians mistakenly callt him Puerto Rican under their breath. Cabrera-Infante chuckled about that and motioned for me to keep on with my lecture. Since I was actually doing a lecture-demonstration I had a huge number of very complicated costume changes. Then, something is lost here. I have a blank.

When I come back for the second half after intermission, a crowd of white thugs, soccer fans, neo-Nazis, who knows the affiliation, bursts through the auditorium doors. I grab Sierra and we run. We swim to an island not far from Santiago de Cuba. Once I reach shore I am breathless, exhausted, and I cannot believe I've lost Sierra in transit, somehow.

Yet Guillermo has this little boy I've never seen before, safe and sound, a stranger's child, hiding with us.

I keep looking for Sierra.

The white hoodlums catch up with us. There is a gigantic tsunami building behind us, at least five meters. We keep running. It is very foggy and cold.

Miguelito Algarin who'd been mingling with the thugs to see what was actually on their minds comes over to the rocks, boulders, where we are hiding. Guillermo and Miguelito embrace. They know each other awready. Miguelito takes a look at this child we're protecting and says nothing. The two decide to take a Jeep and go look for Sierra. They take the little boy baby, too. I mean, they take the boy baby with them.

Guillermo comes back in the Jeep without Miguelito, the baby, or Sierra. He tells me the baby boy was really some guy's baby by some woman he knew while he was in prison. Guillermo was in prison with him and vaguely remembers her from infrequent conjugal visits. Guillermo had gotten out the joint first and raised the baby on his own until he saw the fella and gave him his baby back. They all go away. I can hear Sierra's voice through the pounding surf. Then, I wake up crying.

——— Why is Sierra crying out, Liliane?

——— She's lost. She wants her mother. . . . That's why she's crying.

——— And that's why you're crying, too.

——— No. no. That's not true. My mother wanted me, but Daddy forbid her from me. It wasn't her fault. It wasn't.

——— But, Lili, only one baby can't be located. The other baby is delivered directly to his father's arms.

——— But that was a boy. That was a boy.

——— A baby boy, Lili. A tiny child whose parent was in prison, not much different from where your mother thought she was in her marriage.

——— Who, what you are talking about, is all guys: the lil guy baby, Miguelito, Guillermo, and the guy in jail. What in the world do you think they have to do with me?

——— Well, they're in your dream, Lili.

——— I repeat. They are all guys, males, fellas. They have nothing to do with me. My lil baby person is not locatable after the first two scenes.

——— Liliane, you know as well as I that we do not have dreams where we cease to exist.

——— You mean I was a guy. . . . I was a boy baby? Oh, my God.

——— Worse things could happen.

——— Like what? Oh, my God, I dreamt myself as a baby boy and a man. Jesus, how disgusting. . . . I'd rather die.

——— Lili, listen to me. You dreamt yourself as that lil boy baby abandoned and then saved by men you trust and love very much, men who've delivered you from ethical, ascetic, and spiritual pitfalls, without fail. You dreamt yourself as a child somebody actually made a decision to save, risked lives to get you out of danger. . . .

——— Course, they did. I was a boy.

——— No, Liliane. You were you.

———

——— Liliane, your own warriors saluted you last night.

——— Yeah. Right. As a boy. Some salvation! What're they gonna do when they find out I've got a pussy? Throw me back to the sea?

——— No. Absolutely not. The only one at the bottom of the sea is Sierra, and she wasn't yours to begin with, was she?

——— Of course not, she was Roxie's.

——— And whose are you, Lili? Don't answer too quickly because we've no need for haste, here.

——— I'm, I mean, I'm my own, if I have to belong to somebody.

——— Yes. And who's come to claim you?

——— Nobody. I died in the bottom of the sea. I told you that.

——— No. Sierra died, we think, at the bottom of the sea. Miguel and Guillermo delivered you safely to somebody, who was that, Lili?

———

——— Liliane, can you hear me?

——— *Que tu queres?*

——— *No mucho, chica.* Liliane, don't you feel how protected you were?

——— *No, yo no entiendo nada.*

——— *Sí, tu puedes.* Cabrera-Infante and Algarin took you away in a language that was not dangerous to you and left you with your "true" parent.

——— Cause I was a baby boy.

——— No, because your old-fashioned view of the world only allows boys a second chance. That's why "cause."

——— Wait now, I'm trying to catch up.

——— You don't have to rush, Liliane, they'll wait.

——— Wait for what?

——— For whatever you imagine. There are men who literally are at your beck and call.

——— Stop joshin' me.

——— Liliane, when you didn't even know which baby you were, to be saved, in the first place, they took care of you. I'm sure they'll do anything you want them to do in any dream you ever have. Just remember, you made them up, so they don't take no shit.

——— Is that all?

——— Why, Lili, I think you may be right.

——— So, does that make me a boy?

——— No, that makes us right on time.

——— Well, I'm not quite ready to go yet.

——— Well, what are you planning to do?

——— Oh, I won't bother you, I'm just going to stand out here and see if I can get a whiff of some real testosterone. I wanna be real clear when I explain to the "warriors" in my dreams how it is they sposed to smell. You see?

——— Oh, yes, Lili. I see very clearly, now. Next week.

# "That's Why I Love Her So and Yeah, Yeah, Yeah, I Want to Know" or Why Jackie Wilson Died in Silence

You don't believe it and neither do I, but I been invited to Liliane Lincoln's sixteenth birthday party. Now get to this shit, the bitch is having a slumber party. I guess that means we gonna get a lil bit and go on to sleep. Hey, I know better than that, but what the hell she invite my black ass for? She knows I done peeped her game. Hey, after that sicko job she did on me and Danny in New York, you think I'm gonna trust that bitch a stitch? You got it.

My moms, she's all honored and that. Her baby's gonna stay the night with the daughter of the first black judge we ever heard of. Shit. First black muthafuckah send a niggah to Annondale quick as a guinea. That's all that means to me. Jesus. You'd think them Lincolns was the water Christ walked on. Enough niggahs done drank something magical at Liliane's well to heal the sick for miles. That's what I hear, and I don't interpret nothin' that ain't the God's truth. Don't even raise your eyes to doubt me, now. Have you ever, ever in all your born fawnin'-over-cracker days, known Bernadette to lie. See. Don't make me get upset.

I gotta go to a "slumber party." Jesus. Last time Miss-all-the-race-can-depend-on had a slumber party, didn't nobody come. She came boo-hoo-ing bout prejudice and mean white folks. I say what you expect? Since they might be test-proved-crackers, smart peckawoods, they gonna sleep the night in a niggah bed? Give me a break.

Then give my ass a break, bitch. Shit. I get so tired of her bullshit.

"Surely, Bernadette, you of all people understand, I had to stay with Granville. I've known him most of my life. Our parents are counting on us to . . . further the race, to propel our people to freedom without any dependence on white folks. Don't you understand that? Why can't you see, you of all people, Granville and I are the foundation of a new Negro. It's so clear. We'll never have to depend on white folks for nothing, nothing at all."

I guess we won't ever have to see a redneck again, we'll have our own to cozy up to. Shit. The bitch was totally out of order, out to lunch, but my mama said I had to go. I had to realize what an exceptional person the Lincolns must think I am. Why, I could sleep in their house! Well, you know, I should get me a prayer cloth and snivel in it every hour on the hour that the Lincolns deem me worthy of such "intimacy."

Shit. I get to the place, the house with no number, you just sposed to know it from the roadside, I guess. Anyway, I'm making my way down the path of foot stones so subtle they look like dirt only I could tell they harder cause my feet don't sink into the ground. So I'm most to the door, when Liliane runs out like I just came from the Korean War or something.

"Bernadette, Bernadette. I'm so glad you could make it. My very best friends in the whole world are here. It wouldn't be right without you. It just wouldn't be right." Then she grabbed me up in her arms like I was a child from the television orphan's ad, send twenty dollars, only seventy-nine cents a day, and all that. Oh, I really thought I should be somewhere else. Then, like the goddamn Beverly Hillbillies, these pickaninny heads popped out the doorway one by one: Rose Lynne, well we know bout her, Roxie, Hyacinthe, and I looked to see if there was any more of these fools, but that was it. Thank God.

Well, we started out with all these pizzas we ordered from all over the county: pepperoni, mushrooms, peppers and onions, plain, Sicilian with double cheese, Neapolitan with olives and anchovies. We had more silly-looking white boys looking up our shorty pajamas than Pinoy girls at Clark AFB. Now I know bout that cause both my brothers was hooked up with Filipinas, was bringing them home, and couldn't nobody stop them. You'd think the Negro had enough new blood, but not the way things were going on Liliane's birthday. I was packing them pizzas away and Liliane'd found some beer and some scotch to wash it down, so long as we didn't say nothing to her daddy.

Can you imagine callin' your pa "Daddy" and you sixteen years old? But worse than that, was that Roxie girl cooing Papa like she wasn't an American or somethin'. I was at a total loss for Lollie and Hyacinthe. They were from St. Louis, or so they said. Far as I know they might've been visiting from the Outer Limits. I mean, the South is the South, and my family had relations and cousins down there in the Carolinas, I think, but how young colored girls could be so full of themselves, I'll never understand. Lollie was the one I liked the best, I guess that's cause she had dyed her hair platinum blond and wore it in a real close bob like Twiggy. I liked the look, you know what I mean? Hyacinthe on the other hand must believe that a whole heada nappy hair runnin' wild is what it takes to enter The Kingdom. I have never seen no niggah gal's hair so wild it looked like it must stink. Liliane said I was bein' judgmental, but hell, we are judged by the company we keep.

Since Liliane's mother had passed, the Judge gave her most anything money could buy. It was a shame, too, cause can't nothin' and nobody take Mama's place. Liliane tried to be cool about it, you know, how much she misst her mama. The other girls and I, we made a pact to try to help Liliane really enjoy her sixteenth birthday, since we in a way was all she had to depend on for female stuff. The Judge thought arranging for all of us to come for Liliane's celebration might lessen her loneliness, but I'm here to say couldn't nobody or nothin' calm Liliane's spirit.

Seems like Hyacinthe had a brother was hot shit in Missouri, and found Liliane fetchin', you might say, but those girls was on the phone to Missouri, Nassau, and Mississippi like these boys was right around the corner. I thought Hyacinthe must be feelin' pretty low, cause not one of these silly girls was interested in her at all, only her brother, Sawyer. Lollie and Liliane was beside themselves, talkin' to this fella, but the most ridiculous conversations were between Rose Lynne, Liliane, and Granville. Talkin' to niggahs out of the country, Jesus, I know the Judge hadn't planned all that. He wanted us to keep Liliane's spirits up, not help her get her panties off.

There had always been rumors bout Liliane's mama, S. Bliss, but I never paid that no mind. S. Bliss was nice to me, helping me feel at ease when some big shindig was goin' on. But Liliane braced up real rigid now when anybody referred to her mama, like she was too scared to remember that her mama'd died. All the photos in Liliane's part of the house were of S. Bliss and Liliane picking berries, riding horses, comin' out of church, beamin' at fancy restaurants in foreign places. S. Bliss and Liliane diving from cliffs in Acapulco like any hungry young Mexican boy. Then there were the shots of Liliane and her beloved "daddy" at banquets in his honor, Police Athletic League affairs, and snazzy cocktail parties where Liliane looked more like her daddy's date than his daughter. But you know, it must've been real hard for the Judge and Liliane to come to terms with her mama's death when there was no body to bury or ashes to cherish. It was really awful, you know, tryin' to comfort a girl who doesn't let on that she's hurtin'.

Rose Lynne decided we should call Granville Simeon, like it was her business. Shit, Liliane had let the whole world know that Granville Simeon was hers. He let her know it too, when he insisted that the rest of us get off the extensions, so we couldn't hear what they were sayin'. Hyacinthe teased Liliane that her brother, Sawyer, better not ever hear of a liaison tween her, Liliane, and Granville. Hyacinthe said Sawyer would just as soon cut her face as imagine his Liliane with some no-count West Indian. Lollie suggested immediately that we look at the all-night movies, there was no need for threats and such from boys who weren't really even there with us. I agreed, I didn't like the sounds of these guys' voices, let alone what they were sayin'. Didn't anybody know you didn't haveta let any man talk like he owned you, like we owed them something. For what? So, I could say Sawyer Malveaux thought I was good enough to grace his telephone presence, let alone his actual company.

While Liliane and Rose Lynne were off gabbing with the boys from Nassau to Missouri, Lollie, Hyacinthe, and I were watching the late show. The *Santa Fe Trail,* starring Ronald Reagan and Errol Flynn, with assorted Negro character actors and Ray Massey as John Brown, himself. Lollie was routing for the Abolitionists, Brown and his company of fanatics. Roxie was holdt up in the corner of Liliane's closet like she thought night riders was gonna come to New Jersey. Hyacinthe kept repeating "our plans remain to ourselves, alone" like she was one of John Brown's partisans. I was chugging a beer when I heard a strange squeal jump from Hyacinthe's body. Hyacinthe was distraught that the military strategist for the Abolitionists had ratted on Brown's plans for Harpers Ferry. Hyacinthe was cursin' the TV, jumpin' up and down, screamin': "No, no. They can't stop us. We won't let them stop us. No, no, not in my lifetime." Now, I think I established that Hyacinthe was not all the way there, but taking seriously a Hollywood version of the Emancipation issue was far and away foolish, if you get what I mean. Nothing in that movie was gonna vindicate our pasts, our forebears, our sense of who we are. Hyacinthe should have laughed at those crackers portraying Longstreet, Sheridan, Custer, and Stewart, just like they'd have laughed at us, a bunch of colored girls, saying out loud that crackers not only created a country they stole from other people, but they reaped the riches of the labor of other folks they had stolen. Not only was this a thieves' paradise, but all of us, Lollie, Roxie, Hyacinthe, Liliane, and me, we were living testimony that nobody like us had ever existed before, and nobody had expected we'd be so goddamned hard to kill off.

In the middle of John Brown's speech before he was hanged at Harpers Ferry, Hyacinthe started crying uncontrollably. She ran out the room all over the place like she thought slavers was after her crazy behind. Well, I wanted to see the end of the movie cause I like to know what's up, you see, but Lollie wouldn't stay with me to see whether the predictions of the Indian woman with the stick, drawing spells in the dirt, came true or not. I shouted at her, too: "Lollie, don't you want to see what happened?"

From what seemed like a cave a thousand miles away, Lollie screamed back at me: "They freed the slaves, gal, didn't you hear?" Then I heard foolish-sounding laughter, just like those Southern belles with Jeb Stuart and Jeff Davis. I knew that Roxie, every bit the Tina Turner of the high and mighty, was out there laughing herself to death about me. "They freed the slaves, didn't you hear" bumped up against the walls of the rooms to where I myself was standing: tried to get me, too. To hell with that. To hell with them, too. I gotta sit back here all by myself, while they laugh at me and drink the Judge's liquor, get prissy pussies excited on the phone to Nassau, and generally act the fool.

I could go home. That's what I could do. Call my moms, say things didn't work out the way we'd planned. I want to go home. I'm getting myself together to let these heifers know they ain't the end of the world, when I see Hyacinthe stumbling toward the doorway. I looked at her close, now, cause I know she ain't had no time to be drinkin' or nothin', but she was really fallin' toward me. I was meanin' to go home, now, but nobody else was payin' any mind to this girl. "Hyacinthe, are you all right, huh?" She didn't say nothin' just kept mumblin' and cryin' and movin' toward me. "Hyacinthe, damn. Can you hear me? Are you okay?"

Lord, why did I ask this child anything? Why didn't Lollie or Liliane or Roxie, one of them who knew this girl, get they black behinds back here. "Liliane! Roxie! Lollie!" I was shoutin' for real now, cause Hyacinthe was askin' me crazy shit, I mean, strange shit.

"Do you know where they send us to get our eyes to glow in the dark, Bernadette, I want to know. Bernadette, is that your real name or your slave name? Where is the school for niggahs where they show us how to roll our eyes like this and then like that? Am I getting it right? How's this?"

Now you know sho as I'm breathin', that I don't know nothin' about no rollin' niggah eyes or glowin' niggah eyes, and Hyacinthe is justa practicin' whatever this mess she's talkin' bout. Just now at the point when I know I gotta get the hell outta here, don't ya know here come the slew of drunken banshees, the whole lot of them.

"Oh Lollie, I think Hyacinthe is gone back to slavery times again," Liliane quips very irresponsibly, if you ask me.

Rose Lynne stood still and then ran off somewhere.

"Listen here, I don't think you all should be playin' like that with this girl. She's talkin' all outta her head." And they laughed some more. Hyacinthe is still movin' her eyes around up in the top of her head and mumblin'.

"Hyacinthe, did you find out how our eyes glow in the dark yet? Have you now? Will you show me, too? I want to do it right, now." Then, Roxie got next to Hyacinthe and started to rollin' her eyes, too. Lollie and Liliane commenced to struttin' around like they was some hot shit, right?

"Roxie, your eyes are definitely not glowing adequately. There is no way I could ascertain that you are a bona fide niggah the way you look right now. Now, Hyacinthe here has mastered the art of niggahs in the dark, the glow and the roll." With that said Hyacinthe relaxed, relieved. Now I knew I was goin' home. All these girls was crazy. Liliane looked at me sharply, some nerve. Then she bent over Hyacinthe, who was now sittin', rockin' on the floor. Liliane patted Hyacinthe's head, held her, rocked her. Hyacinthe started to cry again, but this time not crazy like. Lollie and Roxie motioned for me to go with them, like we should leave Hyacinthe to Liliane. As we were creepin' away slowly, I heard Hyacinthe shout out, ". . . That white man talks like he's a friend." That was a line from the movie we were watchin', these bitches think we in a movie, a movie about slavery and niggah eyes. Jesus you know I gotta go home.

"Well, I think we need to call Sawyer, immediately, Lollie, don't you?" Roxie was positioning herself by the phone in the kitchen. Lollie was searchin' cabinets for food, I guess. "Yeah, you are probably right." Lollie found some brandy with fruit in the bottom of it. "You think we could give her some of this? It might quiet her down til we find Sawyer. God only knows where that fool might be."

Before anybody else could say anything, I interrupted: "What in the fuck is wrong with that girl? All you all are crazy as shit."

"There aren't many colored folks who aren't," Roxie said to me so particular, I liked to slapped her damn face. I know I'm not crazy. Lollie put her two cents in first, though, fore I could get my hands on that smartass. "Listen, Bernadette, Hyacinthe has problems," as if a jackass couldn't tell that. Lollie went on, though, "Hyacinthe has episodes of, what shall we call it? Ah, times when bein' a Negro scares her to death. She starts talkin' all that strange slavery talk about glows, and eyes, and big teeth, sometimes, too."

"And, so what are we supposed to do? Why do you all laugh at her so?" I'm mad now. I don't like nobody to make fun of a simple colored girl. "So why were you all laughin'? Tell me."

"We weren't laughing at her, so much as letting her know we know something about the feelings she's having, and that she's not alone. You know, when Hyacinthe is not close to Sawyer she's more likely to have fits like this."

"That's why I said shouldn't we call him, now?" That Roxie just won't give up, you know what I mean.

"Uh, yes. I think, now's a good time to give Sawyer a ring. If he's not at home, which he very well may not be, I've got an emergency number for him in East St. Louis."

"Oh, no, you don't either, Lollie."

"Oh, yes, I most certanly do. We take care of our own where I'm from." Lollie smiled a slow grin, most crazy as Hyacinthe's, took a slug of brandy, called for Liliane and Hyacinthe to come on out to the kitchen. "We're all going to talk to Sawyer, Hyacinthe. Liliane, bring her on, now. I don't want to have to drink all this pear brandy by myself. Where's Rose Lynne. Get her, too."

Jesus Christ. Well. Moms, my mama, told me from the get-go that I was gonna have an experience, but I sure was glad I was not part of the "our own" that Lollie and Roxie looked after.

"Hey, Bernadette, aren't you goin' to have a drink with us?" Roxie asked. "If you sip a little, makes rollin' your eyes much easier," Liliane joked.

"Liliane, you quit mocking Bernadette, you hear. Just leave her alone. She's not used to us, just yet," Rose Lynne said with a silly smile.

I looked round the kitchen. We was all there in our nighties like in *Seventeen,* but it was only our pajamas let me know I wasn't as mad as Hyacinthe and the others. Then, I changed my mind when Roxie went around the table like a half-dead chicken: "Hyacinthe, we got Sawyer on the phone for you. He's wanting to talk to you. Right now." How Hyacinthe grinned and bucked them eyes with glee. Now, you know, I ain't never bucked my eyes like that and don't wanta know how, neither. Lollie spied my attitude, started singin' with Hyacinthe's head on her shoulder:

> *"That's why. That's why*
> *that's why I love her so,*
> *That's why that's why*
> *I love her so and yeah, yeah, yeah*
> *I want the world to know."*
>
> —JACKIE WILSON

# Room in the Dark XI

——— So what have we here?

——— A woman too tired to talk, that's what.

——— Not only too tired to talk, but too tired, apparently, to get here on time or to pay her bills on time.

——— I still owe you money? I thought I paid money last week.

——— That was three weeks ago and that was "some" money, not the amount owed.

——— Oh.

——— Well, what are you going to do about all this?

——— All this?

——— Yes, you've been late for the last five sessions; tired; and fairly unengaged as well.

——— Oh, so now I must be perky and smiling as well as

witty and perceptive? Fuck you. [She throws her hat at him.]

——— Liliane, you must never do that again. Only verbal exchanges are permitted: no acting out; no physicality.

——— Gee, I'm sorry. It's just that I don't want to do anything but work. I don't wanta eat, fuck, come here or anywhere else.

——— Then, you should be able to pay your bills, if you are working so much.

——— Damn. You are having a real hard time with this, aren't you?

——— No, I'm having a hard time understanding you right now. You are giving me very little to work with.

——— Welcome to the club.

——— Lili, isn't this a bit melodramatic?

——— If you say so. I'm tired of fighting. I'm tired of defending myself, believe whatever the fuck you want, okay? You want me to go?

——— No, and I want you to pay me. And I want you to acknowledge who you are angry with and why you are coming late to do our work and refusing to pay me.

——— What in the hell are you talking about?

——— We are talking about this episode of acting out that you're doing.

——— Oh, I see.

——— Do you really, Lili?

——— Well, no, not exactly. I don't really understand.

——— Well, let's review a bit. . . . You started being late

with regularity when we discovered the connection between your mother and Roxie.

——— I did?

——— Yes, you did. I didn't mention it then, because you were very intent on remembering everything you could.

——— And now you think I'm running away?

——— What do you think?

——— I told you. I've been working myself to death, that's what. Look, look, see what I've been doing. I've been working and trying to understand, I have. I swear, my whole being is involved in this. [She pulls out a small book.] This is our book, me and Mommy, I mean, Sunday Bliss. She wrote me some letters that I never told you about cause I wanted to make them something, anything I could hold, before I shared her with anybody. She's my mother. I love her. I want some of her for myself, that's all.

——— That does not explain being late or failure to pay . . . unless since you're growing close to S. Bliss again, your fury at her so-called death is directed at me.

——— You are out of your mind, you know that?

——— No, I'm just trying to figure out what's going on here.

———

———

——— Well, did you want to see what I've been doin'?

——— If that's what you want, that's what I want.

——— [She opens the little book eagerly, yet delicately.] See, these are parts of the letters Mommy sent me that I glued onto pages here and then drew or painted around them my feelings. That's why I figured we'd have a book of our own, something we made together.

——— Even though you didn't do it together?

——— We did do it together! She sent me what she had and I added what I had. Then, *voilà,* we have our book.

——— But she hasn't seen the book, just like she hasn't seen you.

——— Oh, damn you, shut up! Just shut up. I thought she was dead. I thought she didn't love me. I thought she was lying somewhere in the Atlantic Ocean like dead slaves and runaways. Mother as an abstract idea is not foreign to me, you stupid muthafuckah. We made this book, you hear. My mommy and me made this book from pieces of our lives that *I,* Liliane Lincoln, put together. Do you understand that?

——— I understand as beautiful as this book is with its lace and watercolors, its singed edges and perfumed corners, it is made up of torn fragments and elusive memories that are yours alone.

——— But the crux of the little book is my mother's letters, her letters to me.

——— Maybe so, but the book is yours.

——— You got that right. I put my name on everything I make. I sign everything.

——— What did your mother, S. Bliss, sign? Or was she such a metaphysical configuration that she left no visible traces of her presence?

——— Why are you being so horrid? My mother left me. That's what she left. I'm her signature. I'm her emblem. Don't you see?

——— No, I'm not sure I do.

——— Well, you should read the *Book of Ruth* in the Bible.

——— Why should I read the *Book of Ruth,* Lili?

——— See, this is what is wrong with "humanism."

——— Lili . . .

——— Okay. Naomi told Orpah and Ruth to go on their way, to go back to their families because she as a mother-in-law had nothing to offer them anymore.

——— But I understand that Ruth refused to leave Naomi and lived happily ever after.

——— You are missing the whole point as it applies to me.

——— And how does it apply to you, Lili?

——— Well, my mommy, S. Bliss, knew it was better for us to see her dead than with a white man.

——— How is that, Lili?

——— Cause you could forgive somebody for dying, but not for runnin' off with one of them. I would have been, oh my God, I would have been "blacklisted" of all things. It's like having a baby out of wedlock. The black bourgeoisie takes these things very seriously.

——— Are you saying a whole community would have turned against a child?

——— We were never children, we were the future of the race.

——— Liliane, you are carrying around a tiny little book full of shreds of letters from a mother you haven't seen in twenty years, yet you want me to believe that there is no significance in this?

——— No. I'm mad. I'm very mad.

——— Who are you mad at?

——— Right now, I'm mad at you, but I'm mad at Daddy and the black people who were our friends, but I'm most especially mad at this goddamned country which imagines that we don't exist, don't have loved ones and histories and dreams for our children. I'm mad about watching our daily lives stamped out like so many fireflies.

———

——— Oh, you'll never understand if I don't tell you.

——— Yes, that's true.

——— My mommy didn't want to leave, but she had no place to take me with Mr. Rothen . . . whatever his name is. You can't take a child somewhere that doesn't exist. And Daddy was so sure women were decorative afterthoughts; the substance of Mommy though always alluring was also something to be hidden.

——— That would be hard, it seems to me, to hide S. Bliss.

——— That was impossible.

——— So what are you hiding now, Lili?

——— I'd like to say, "Oh, nothin'," but I guess I'm hiding all the years I wish I'd had with her, but not with that man.

——— So, like your daddy you want S. Bliss all to yourself, too?

——— Yeah, I guess so, but Mommy'd already taught me about beauty. She'd already shown me so much of what was precious in me. Ha, I couldn't destroy that no matter how many tackhead fools I fucked. Jesus, this is monumental.

——— Or diversionary. We haven't established why you are continually late and refuse to pay me.

——— Oh, that's simple.

——— Really?

——— Yeah. I don't want to talk about my mother disappearing, so the later I come the less I have to talk.

——— Yes.

——— And see I've been making these books from my mother's letters, but it's a limited edition, one of a kind really, and nobody wants to buy them, so I have no money.

——— But you are working all the time and you have no money?

——— Yeah. See, nobody wants a pretty book that's full of enough information to make you care but not enough information to want to keep it under your pillow at night.

——— That presents us with a dilemma, doesn't it? How are you going to pay me?

——— Well, to be quite honest, I thought I'd see if you wanted to buy these lil books, three, I've made so far. Then, I'd give you that money and you'd have my mother in your pocket. They're really very tiny.

——— I'm not sure that's where I'd like to have your mother, but we are absolutely out of time.

——— Oh, my goodness.
——— Liliane, I want these matters addressed next time we meet.
——— Yes, massa.
——— But do not forget, the women in the time of Judges said, "She is worth more to you than seven sons."
——— I can go home with that.

# There's No Use Cryin' "Forever" or Hyacinthe Returns from a Very Blue Holiday for Real B(l)ack at Ya

I guess I can't stay crazy forever. "Play crazy" is what Aurelia call it. Aurelia's gotta name for everything. I wonder what she calls Lollie. I don't even know what I call Lollie: my friend, my confidante, my ace boon coon, my sister? See I can't start to make lists like that cause listing things gets me all revved up and I don't make sense to other people, so they say I'm crazy. I get mad at them and then I might really seem crazy. But as far as I'm concerned, I don't know many Africans and descendants thereof who ain't halfway crazy. Plus, going crazy is so startling and scary to them once they realize their true state of mind, that they pretend sanity, much as they can. Now me, I've been crazed so long and so intensely, I'm really good at it, comfortable, you might say.

Sawyer was outta his gorgeous mind, you know. Thought those lovely lean fingers and rapid-fire brain could protect his behind from what Langston callt "the ways of white folks." Only thing ever protected me was my brother and my madness. That's why Aurelia says she's going to work on me now. "Lollie's getting married, so my nut is off my hands. I can devote myself to you, dear Hyacinthe." That's what she said. She did. If my mother could look at me and only see Sawyer, or niggers, I guess I'd be offended, but I'm not. My mama, Bienaimée Malveaux, never got used to the idea, the fact, that she had colored children! I have never been able to figure out what she imagined was gonna fall from her body but some niggahs. Well, it don't matter cause I'm living proof that ignoring niggahs doesn't make us go away.

But it is true that Lollie's getting married. Of all people to be a blushing bride. Lollie is the closest colored to Jean Harlow that I ever encountered. Blond as a summer moon and bold like a colored Miss Kitty on *Gunsmoke*. Bienaimée always swore wouldn't nobody ever, ever marry the likes of Lollie. Yet once again she's dead wrong, incorrect, in error, mistaken, off target, waylaid, mislaid, misled, fuckin' stupid bitch, dumb twat, ignorant jackass, stank pussy, fool. Oh, see, I tol' you, I cannot make lists. No lists. They won't let me outta here if I make lists like that. They won't ever let me outta here. I wanna go to Lollie's wedding. I want Aurelia to he'p me. That's how she says it. He'p me. Aurelia believes I am playing at being crazy.

"Now, Hyacinthe, I'm only going to say this once. You cannot stop living on account of Sawyer, your brother, made some injudicious choices in his own life. You not joined at the hip, if you get me. Now, you are going to do what these folks here ask you to do, you are going to stay out the Quiet Room, and you are coming to Lollie's party and I'm going to marry you on away from your mama just like I got Lollie on her merry way. Thank you, Jesus." That's what she said.

I think Aurelia might actually like me a little bit. I know Lollie loves me, but sometimes I think Lollie loves me like you take to a stray of some kind of a dog, maybe a man. But it's just I could never stand white folks, let alone how they treat us. That's why I'm here. That's why they say crazy cause I want to fuck white folks up, break they necks. But I'm a girl. Well, hell, I've always been a girl and my brother was more beautiful than me, lovelier, smooth, soft, delicate, brown, long, limber, suave, warm, kissable, kissing, kisses, kiss me, Sawyer. No. No. Stop. I never had to kill like my brother. I'd wake to blood and torn human organs every morning until I learned to take the moans of our folks who were dying in my body. Then, when I screamed it was 10,000 mad, anguished niggahs they threw in the Quiet Room. "The Quiet Room," like that scares me. How you gonna scare ten thousand dead niggahs who've seen the bottom of the Mississippi River, the floor of ravines outside Springfield, hid behind stalactites and stalagmites in coves near Jeff City, holed up in corrals by the Kentucky border. Somebody believe they gonna scare me, when I'm fulla alla that? Well, come again, as they say in these parts, I could take it.

Ever since Sawyer died, was killed, shot in the head, murdered, butchered, knocked off, hit, gotten rid of, executed, shot, taken out, blown away, blown away, blown away. Stop! Stop. Let me get my breath. I haven't been able to put white folks in their place. I know what the cops said. They said it was niggahs what killt Sawyer, but I know Sawyer was dead long 'fore those so-called niggahs got to him. Sawyer was being assassinated from the time he was born and my crazy mother,

Bienaimée, was totally dumbfounded bout how she birthed these "niggahs." From the first time he opened his eyes, took her bronze nipple in his mouth until he was taking me and Liliane to East St. Louis, Sawyer knew nothing but disdain, contempt, and envy.

"Whatta pretty niggah he is." You betcha forlorn cracker life, that's the truth. "Is that your brother, Hyacinthe?" "He's whatever you imagine that he feels like accommodatin', darlin'." That's the way it was. That's the way it was. That's the way it was til Lili.

My brother met Lili on Lollie's front porch. He said she was just lolling about on Lollie's porch. The sound of it seemed as exciting to me as the actuality. Lolling, Lollie, Lili. The sounds were intoxicating, he said. My Lili, I call her that cause she never thought I was crazy, least no more crazy than she was. Plus, I know, don't matter how I know, but I know Lili was whatever my brother wanted when he wanted and I know she'd always thank him for such opportunities cause he told me so. Oh, don't get all beside yourself! My brother never allowed anyone or anything to give him more pleasure than he'd delivered to them. I guess that means we don't have to feel sorry for Lili, huh?

I'm here now where butterflies, bees, and garter snakes make their home, ephemeral, transient creatures like me: they delight and disappear. Liliane taught me that. We come and go. We provoke laughter or desire and we disappear. Liliane was like a sister to me cause she loved my brother and she loved me. Sawyer woulda died for her, but he never got the chance. White folks, no niggahs, hunted him down. That's not true, but I had to say that so they'll let me outta this goddamn place. Sawyer got killt, somebody blew his ass away, cause he was a niggah 'n whoever was payin' em was not. Didn't no black somebody send my brother to his grave. Was a brother up for sale, looking for somebody to caress his arms, shoulders, run palms down his thighs, and tongues over his balls and deep, deep down in his throat. Silly niggahs'd do anything for money. If he'd wanted to, my brother, Sawyer, could've paid niggahs to . . . oh let's say their tongues would meet somewhere; the center of his groin, uhhhmmmm. Unless Liliane introduced herself to the situation. Then, oh my God, Sawyer and Liliane had their way with the world; the world as they knew it.

And thank God I was always a part of it. I was always included in anything Sawyer and Lili did: everything, everywhere. This is not really as perverse as you think. Lili visited me here in this awful place with locked wards and room inspections at most inappropriate times. My sense of her is chaste. Liliane gave what she gave to Sawyer, and the rest of us will never really know what that was cause Lili and Sawyer never got all we could give them. Consequently, he's dead and she's gone.

Query: Is Aurelia gonna set Lili straight, too? We could all go off to the chapel together. I'll get a big big white lace dress with a hoop skirt and bundle my dreads on the tip-top of my head. Aurelia knows better than to make me cut my dreads. That's another reason I'm here. I let my hair go back, get nappy, turn back, wrinkle, crinkle, twist, curl, swirl, oh shit. I've gotta stop these lists. I don't really know if they are listening to me or not. There are two-way mirrors and microphones in here, I'm sure. It's a teaching hospital and whatever they didn't find out about us during slavery and circus tours, they gonna find out now. That's what they think, but when Lili came to visit she told me even when they think they know they don't know. Lollie says it is not the worst thing in the world that I imagine I'm cutting white folks' throats during pleasant banter at the lunch table. Has Aurelia seen to Lollie? That's what I want to know.

Liliane and I, we see things. I haven't really been anyplace, since, well, since Sawyer was murdered, was killt. Okay, I stopped. Now, listen to me. I have not been any goddamn where 'cept places Lili took me. Lili took me everywhere with her. I went to Haiti, Cuba, Taos, London, Aix-en-Provence, Matamoras, even New York City. I wish I knew where the yacht S. Bliss died on was. I'd take Lili there. Then we could have a real funeral and let her mama rest in peace, but I remember, now, wasn't no boat or body, was a negress run off with a cracker is what. Yet and still, my Lili, my Liliane, shared anything and everyone she had with me. I ought to know, I've been here a long, long time. Gimme a second. All I have to do is dig down in these drawers a bit and you'll see. Why here's Liliane and that Granville character. Lemme set up on my bed, so I can relax a little. What I mean to say is that Lili sent me, actually sends me, drawings, photographs, papier-mâché images of who is in her life. She makes me feel like I was actually there, I could touch em, and smell em, and, sometimes, I love em: Lili's friends, Lili's nemesis, niggahs what kicked Lili's ass, is what she let me experience with her.

My social workers chastise me constantly cause I line my walls, the walls of my room, with Lili's drawings. "Why Miss Malveaux, you know you've never been any of these places;

why you've never even been out of my sight for more than eight hours." When my nurses talk like this, I don't say anything cause they don't know no better. Let me show you. That's what Lili says, "Let me show you."

See, looky here. There's Rose Lynne, Roxie, Lollie, Bernadette, and me all straddling that Granville boy from somewhere outta here, you know what I mean. We are remarkable, ain't we? Look at us. Just as fine as fine can be. Just as . . . susceptible to murder as anybody else. Awright, you wanna dispute me. Okay. Here's Lili's take on Roxie and Tony. All you gotta do is look at these drawings, okay? See, love.

Lili sent me these drawings with the following note: "Hey scrunch. I never saw people so in love before, I knew you'd want to know. It's Roxie and some Cuban beau she found over here. My arms hurt, my back is bout to break, but we gonna bring in a sugar harvest to be talked about sho as you born. Love, Lili."

Liliane was in Escambray with all those hard-nosed counterrevolutionaries, who claimed they were patriots. But Jose Martí or Bolívar didn't seek no solace with no white Cubans from Escrambray, be like asking Bull Connor do he want a black daughter. Anyway, Lili let poor Roxie, who didn't know much of nothin' bout nothin', Lili let Roxie linger in this Latin's arms. Now, I'm not saying that Tony was not a hot prospect, but I can admit that Tony was a white Latin when he met Roxie and we all know he was still a white Latin when he left Roxie: bludgeoned, stabbed, bleeding, dyin', strangled, beat, shot, deformed, stomped, broke, twisted, left, left, left for dead. He left her for dead and I have here in front of me my friend's drawings of how beautiful Roxie might have looked, how full of hope for her and those children she let us be. So, Lili is not protecting me. I am no different than any other black colored Negro person. I want my friend back. I want my brother back. I want crackers to stop killin' us. I wanta gun; a .25, a 9-millimeter, a AK-47, a Tech-9. I want to see somebody else die. One after another like my friends died. One for one. I want to go outta here and see more than spilt blood and white folks.

"Oh Aurelia, I didn't know you were here!" I am slipping my drawings from Liliane under my thigh, but Aurelia sees me.

"Why, Hyacinthe, I know these young folks. They're friends of Lollie, as I recollect."

"Yes, m'am, they probably are," I said under my breath.

Liliane went off with Jean-René, see there he is, as black as a delta berry, but his folks didn't want my Lili cause wasn't no "color" pedigree on her. Lili was same for them as she was for us, a colored gal strange looking and no more likely to give up the black in her than she'd give up her soul. So she stopped drawing pictures of him, though he must have been a beauty, must've been. Then, I've got these old Polaroids of Danny and his new wife, old wife by now. Lili sent me drawings of his hands on her legs, how he kissed her without ever really touching her. Well, that's what she said. Besides the drawings from Rose Lynne's wedding to the SONY executive and Granville's inauguration as prime minister of somewhere don't even approach the grandeur of Bernadette's wedding to that king from Swaziland or Togo, or Botswana. They think I'm crazy, but Liliane and Victor-Jésus actually secreted *indepentisto* fugitives in their house. In their house? That's a federal crime. That means I've gotta admit there are more niggahs speak Portuguese than English. What am I gonna do about that? What am I gonna do about that? I don't know. I repeat, I don't know, but I do know Lili can draw all this, all plain and clear for me and you. I know that. Lili can paint my craziness. She can paint it, build it, hammer and beat it outta nothin'. We came from outta nowhere and my friend, Liliane, can make that somewhere I could go home to. Whenever I want, anytime I want. Zoom really loved her, I think. Victor-Jésus loved her. S. Bliss probably loved her too, but I've gotta look through these watercolors, before I say. Oh hell, I loved Liliane, too: loved, cared, cherished, adored, craved, desired, blessed, yes, blessed. We all were blessed, to have the privilege to love her, Liliane, anybody's colored child, anybody's daughter, just like me. Stop. Stop. You are too close.

# Room in the Dark XII

——— I really want to clear something up today. I can't quite figure this out. I really can't.

———

——— Oh, it's going to be another one of those days, huh?

——— What sort of a day do you mean, Liliane?

——— The kind of day that means I talk-talk and you peruse, contemplate, and don't open your mouth to say a thing: that kind.

——— Oh, but Lili, if you talk-talk we can probably clear up some of what's puzzling you.

——— I certainly hope so. I've been feeling conflicted, or afflicted, as my grandma might've said.

———

——— You see, now that I know about this huge charade my parents created so the two of them could have their worlds just the way they wanted, I'm really mad. I'm fuckin' pissed, actually. How dare they? Make me half an orphan, and then not an orphan. S. Bliss is a perfect wife and she's a slut. Daddy is a colored King Solomon, but he's really a Paraguayan fascist who disappears people, more specifically, his wife. Even thinkin' about this makes my blood rush to my cheeks. Oh! I am so mad at them!

——— That's understandable, Lili. They made some decisions that changed the contours of your life significantly.

——— "Changed"? You must mean warped, distorted, or something like destroyed, right?

——— I think you know that I choose my words very carefully.

——— And you think telling a child her mother's died is just "a change in the contours" of my life. Don't make me laugh.

——— I don't hear you laughing, Liliane.

——— Damn straight.

———

——— I've been thinkin' and I've been thinkin'.

——— Yes.

——— There's no goddamned reason she can give me for leaving in the first place, and on top of that staying gone all my life, all my life. What muthafuckah could be worth all that? And a white man? No wonder my daddy threw her ass out. We don't need no bitch gettin up from suckin' some cracker cock to come kissin' on us. Shit. No.

——— So, now you understand your father's position?
——— I understand that I'm mad.
——— Oh, I can see that, Lili, but a while ago you were mad with both of your parents.
——— You got that right.
——— I might be right on the money, but I think you might be angry with Parnell and Sunday Bliss Lincoln for different reasons.
——— Sunday Bliss Rothenstein, Rothenstein, shit. She walks out the door, leaves me behind, goes off with her lover to start a new life, and I have to live with her over and over again, because all I had was memories. I had memories and pictures. Memories and stories I'd tell sometimes. That's all I had. And she, that bitch had a whole life . . . and I wasn't in it.
——— Well, not physically.
——— Hey, I'm in no mood to play around here. If I was a part of her interior worlds I sure would've made her call, just once. Send a train ticket. Meet me at a friend's house. She could have done a whole lotta things. [Liliane starts to cry.] What the hell are you lookin' at?
——— A young woman who is as hurt as she is furious.
——— Fuck. This is too much for me. I always heard "S. Bliss is somethin' else," but I'm not ready for this. I'm just not.
——— Well, if you're not ready, you don't haveta try to be.
——— What?
——— Lili, you can make adjustments in your life, about

your mother or your father, at your own pace. They dashed about in your childhood with abandon. You don't have to allow that again. You can have as little or as much contact as you desire.

——— See, my head is hurtin' me now.

——— I can see how the Lincolns could be a "headache."

——— What if she doesn't like me?

——— Now how would that happen?

——— My father raised me. She left his behind: too controlling, too rigid. What if she sees him every time she looks at me?

——— Liliane, it'd be hard for anybody to see a sixty-year-old man when they look at you.

——— But, don't you see? I don't know what I mean to her, or meant to her. Shit. When I took Sierra to Mississippi to Roxie's parents, I thought I was going to die. I . . . si . . . My heart was . . . achin'.

——— Liliane, we don't know that your mother didn't feel like she was dying. We don't know she didn't have a broken heart or a gaping emptiness when she left you.

——— You're tryin' to make this easier, aren't you?

——— There's no way we can make any of this easier, I'm sorry to say.

——— But it's just that nobody was thinkin' about me. Daddy has his principles, his honor. And she got her freedom, I guess.

——— Does she still raise orchids, Lili?

——— I don't know, probably. Maybe not, though, cause . . .

——— Cause she's got one flower that still needs tending to, I think.

——— I know you're not referring to me?

——— I most certainly am.

——— Aw, sometimes you are sweet, but this is one wore-out posey over here.

——— Well, what's that like?

——— What? Being wilted? [She laughs.]

——— Yes.

——— Humm. I could probably do better if I tell you this dream. It's one of those dreams that get me up thinkin' I should do whatever I imagined I should be doin' in the dream. You know, I get up and go to meet people I talked to in my dreams. Hell, I get up to fix em somethin' to eat.

——— And who were you feeding last?

——— I wasn't feedin' anybody, actually. I was makin' a mess. A big mess. [She giggles.] I was makin' a big goddamn mess. I was. I really was.

——— Yes, Lili, painters are fairly anal.

——— Oh, you hush up and listen to my dream.

——— I'm right here.

——— Well, we're in the house I grew up in with two floors and a porch, but I'm downstairs in one of my mother's very sexy evening gowns, shoes, her rhinestone heels, and a small purse. I've gobs of lipstick and powder on, stirring a large concoction of every liquor I could find in a beautiful punch bowl. There is some band playing in the kitchen. I'm tempted to say Hank Ballard and the Midnighters.

——— All right. Say that then.

——— Yes. Yes. I think I am preparing for guests cause I go to Mommy's first greenhouse and pick some of her orchids. I put a few in my hair and the rest in the punch and the lapels of The Midnighters. Just when I feel everything is ready, I hear Mommy coming down the stairs, shouting at me: "Liliane, what are you doin'?" I turn around to check everything and The Midnighters disappear. I pour a lil punch into the crystal cup for me and Mommy. She gets to the landing of the stairway and I say: "Why, S. Bliss, I'm so glad you could come." Well, from the look on her face I could tell she was horrified. "Liliane, what in the hell have you done to yourself?" I start to feel a bit less beautiful. "I was getting ready to entertain some friends," I say. Mommy starts to notice my decorations: her flowers and my punch. She approaches me with tears welling in her eyes. "Oh my God, Lili, my flowers. You picked my flowers." Thinkin' that now Mommy needed a drink, I handed her some punch, my punch. She took a sip, looking very bewildered, and then spit it out, almost in my face. "Look what you've done. You lil bitch." I start to cry. The flowers in the punch seem sodden and dreary. My dress is too big. I think my makeup is smeared with tears. Mommy turns away from me and throws the punch bowl, all my condiments and things on the floor. "Who in the hell do you think could drink this mess, huh? Tell me." I wake up shaking and very frightened.

——— I'm sure that frightened a little girl.

——— But my mother loved parties, dancin', and, well, entertainin'.

——— But she wasn't entertainin', was she?

——— No, she was my guest. That's why I was all dressed up.

——— But what was special to her, in the dream, was not a little girl's fantasies of growing up, but her flowers.

——— And the mess I made.

——— Well, little girls are unpredictable, fantastical, messy creatures who need their messes and dreams validated.

——— Not spit back in their faces.

——— That's right, Liliane. Your mommy is the one who turned your life into a bitter "concoction" where precious flower petals wilted and the music disappeared.

——— But it was my dream, right?

——— Yes, but for better or worse, S. Bliss is very real.

——— Oh shit. Know what I just realized? Hank Ballard sang the original "Twist." S. Bliss sure put a twist on my life.

——— That she did, Lili. It's time.

——— Shit. You can't even smell orchids. At least I smell like Liliane.

——— Undoubtedly.

Lollie Struts Her Stuff
Thru
"The Sea of Love"
or
the Brides of Funkenstein
Catch the Bouquet

Well, all I could say was they was a-reelin' and a-rockin'; the church was bout to get on up and shout hallelujah! To my mind, these colored folks never left what they came from: alla Lollie's folks was reekin' of slavery times, though they'd fight you to the death to say otherwise. But what could they say to me? I'm always gointa be more black than where they at. I'm Victor-Jésus María, the forever foreign brother, you know one of them Africans stole by somebody other than the folks what stole you and your pitiful behind, like was some kinda diminutive Tarzan pulled from the jungle of a pyschotic brain, soaked in formaldehyde and white women's sweat for no less than four days. I know this cause I am the only one of my kind in sight, in any direction at all. I was a bigger mystery than Lili's poor dead beau, Sawyer Malveaux.

I haven't told a soul, not even Liliane that I plan to capture

Sawyer's ghost mingling with the wedding party as I document Lollie's marriage extravaganza. This all seems rather incestuous to me. Lollie's marrying Lili's old boyfriend, Granville, whose brother is sniffin' after that crazy bitch, Hyacinthe, who's Sawyer's survivin' sister. Lord, this is wild, ain't it? Oh, but we mustn't forget that Roxie's not here, either. Being colored is definitely dangerous, you know what I mean? Two members of the wedding get killed, not die, get straight up and murdered, and as Lollie says, if it can happen to her it could happen to anybody, just ordinary Negro people.

"Lollie, Lollie, please, I wanta take your picture please, Lollie."

*"We don't know something that's troubling us is*
*weighing on this legend coming our way*
*But think of us, he did*
*Dream for some of us, he did*
*Fight for all of us, oh, he did that, too,*
*And care for us always, whether we came with*
*Sweet potato pigs and sweet voices or*
*Pedigrees that could fly all the way to Dakar.*
*We could feel it in the breeze, catch it in his eyes,*
*Joy, faith, gumption, this man who walked among us*
*Knew the people could fly."*

This Lili recites to me while I'm documenting Lollie's nuptials. "Sweetheart, isn't that a bit gruesome for something like this?"

"Oh, no! Hyacinthe wrote that years ago when Sawyer died. I was just thinkin' about him. I don't know why." Lili's gaze eclipsed the preened and not too proper opulence of Auntie Aurelia's gardens and sped off to some juke joint in southern Illinois. It's odd, lookin' at whole families of Negro people, how we can see who belongs to who, *a quien es quien, tu sabes?* All kinds of spirits show up or come out, with who knows what on their minds and hearts, when we marry, give birth, die, even if we just get a little more of ourselves from ourselves. I'm Victor-Jésus María, a consistent and compassionate marvel of creation. To say the least, I am able to guide the lost and unrecovered gems of our folks to landscapes more appropriate to our nature. Ha, that's right: my photos. In my worlds no persons of color ever look crazy. *Mi tierra.* The land is all guys like me and Zapata ever wanted to give back to us. So, the land I give us is *un poquito,* metaphorical. If you was as black as me, inhabiting lands inhospitable to white folks, *en realidad,* ain't all that damn bad. Don't worry, even good old Jorge Luis had to make up some "wheres" somebody could only dream of experiencing. But like I always tell my Lili, "I see you everywhere I look. Even if I close my eyes, I still can't help lookin' at you, *querida.*"

I tell *mi morena dulce* a lot of things, as you know. I have to secure our territory, not unlike Emiliano Zapata or Miles Davis. And those communal activities, even Lollie's wedding, bless her peroxided head, these rituals are opportunities for the continuation of clans, dreams, fields of fancy, and realms of the spirits. We all know that zombies and still-born infants traipsed from Jacmel, Cap Haitien, to Port-au-Prince to free Haiti. *Pero, sabemos tambien,* some of those same spirits and never-born souls came from the hills to assist Duvalier as well.

Maybe here by the Mississippi, during one or more of our

so clandestine colored events, the old spirits will come out to celebrate with us, *como un bembee:* we dance and we get stronger. We dance and we can go to war. *Pero, no tu preocupes.*

We're here to see what's up with Lili, Lollie, and *su gente libre, su gente bella.*

Ah-ha. Here's Lollie with her mother, Aurelia, going up the gangplank to some riverboat cafe for the wedding rehearsal dinner. Smooth freckled cheeks, the same. The smiles ripe with lust, the same. The clouds rolling by the sun dim the light enough for their eyes to stay we open, determined and hopeful that this will be Lollie's definitive debut to "society" and Aurelia's greatest accomplishment. Eventually, Lollie will lose some of her mother's guile, release the not so hardened Lollie who is a daughter of the river spirit Erzulie. There she is with the shape of a mermaid, tussled blond braids and Eartha Kitts's grin, to dine, to fête: a bride for the gods.

Oh, I forgot. My Liliane, let alone Lollie, would be so terribly, terribly angry with me, if I forgot to say what they were wearing. I, myself, Victor-Jésus María, had nothing to do with this. I'm always interested in the tastes of my subjects. *Tu m'entiendes?* Floral patterned silk organza dresses, low-cut bodice and hot pink satin platform shoes. Hey, this is Lollie's affair. I'm tellin' you the colors and stuff, so you have a sense of the evening. I think Aurelia was telling Lollie to watch her gutter mouth cause West Indians are seriously old-fashioned.

Well, here's a mystery. I think this is a close-up of Sunday Bliss's eyes; *desaparecida* of our generation. Liliane never mentioned that her mother's eyes are the color of lilacs. Yes, lilacs with veins of white hot steel. Even now I'm drawn to her, feel her brush by me. Damn. *Pobrecita,* Lili, no wonder you're such a *loquita,* growing up with a mama like that. What a fox! No, I'm not entertaining any notions of leaving my Lili. No, Lili's eyes are deep warm browns that glow or dim, gleam and twinkle with warmth, with alla her. This Bliss woman steals the sun for herself and leaves the rest of us in shadows. *Pero,* she still only has one pair of eyes, so it ain't magic.

I really like this one: Lollie and everybody, all her wedding maids, were on the upstairs back terrace in their slips. (We'd just come in from tearin' up the town, the towns and country, if you will.) I'm really trying to do my job, capturing everything about Lollie's wedding. I stand behind the French doors: "Are you all decent yet?" There is a lot of typical female giggling. "Have you ever known us to be decent?" That's Lollie. "You wanta whole lotta decent or jus' a lil bit?" I think that's Bernadette. So I say: "Only what you can handle." "Then, bring it on, *negrito*" and you know that was Lili as well as I do.

Imagine my surprise to see Roxie's spirit just as lively under sky beginning to breathe the light of day. Roxie before Tony, before Sierra, before any kind of madness besides white folks, was truly the quintessential belle. She took me by my hand to each of Lollie's court. Ramito stood on the neighbor's roof, serenading them all. Bernadette and Lili pouring Mumm's Extra Brut champagne over Lollie's head. Rose Lynne looking off to the sunrise, wishing on a morning star, a starlit *Taino.* Perhaps, strolling by, Hyacinthe watches the doors, anxiously. By the railing, Roxie's spirit flirts with me in Elizabeth Taylor's slip from *Cat,* offering her friends many sunrisings, *conjuntos siempre:* together always.

How I caught Sawyer Malveaux in his tailored suit and wickedness, *yo no say.* But there he is in the door to the cathedral, peering over Sierra in her tiara of orchids and roses, protecting the child who was not protected. Formidable, though evanescent, Sawyer gestured to Roxie to come from behind the portico. Sierra's head just reaches Sawyer's thighs. Her flower basket tips a bit, when Roxie bends to kiss her daughter. Sierra turns toward that energy. Her flowers tumble gracefully to the ground. Worried, she looks up. *N'importa hija.* Sawyer and Roxie are not mad. They won't hurt you. No one in the picture I took will ever hurt you, *niña.*

One of those nights down here with Lollie and Granville, all the fellas went on a spree, if you know what I mean. We headed off for East St. Louis in honor of Sawyer, in honor of free enterprise, black business, outlaws, and revelry. We didn't know each other as well as our *compadres,* but, then we each took some gettin' used to. It's not that I don't care for Granville. He's just *un poco,* huh, elitist, is the word. So what is new with this bunch, *sí?* Anyway, with me and Thayer being the working "artist" types, we sort of lead the pack. Then that French dandy (don't tell my Lili I said this), but Jean-René is truly a difficult son of a bitch. Every other word out of his mouth is, "And what do you mean?" I was ready to tell him to take his black ass back wherever he came from if he couldn't speak English, but I know, I know, I caught myself before such a grand faux pas, *tu sabes.*

Still, even Jean-René thought it was funny when Thayer pointed out that we all know "the girls" or "the bitches" depending on who was around, better than we knew each other. We'd heard of each other before we ever laid eyes on our variously magnificent selves. That's actually how we came up with the idea that we leave those women at home and go on out and be men, for a night at least. I must say, however, the "mighty" Mississippi at night did not take my breath away, a awful-lookin' mess of a river. It did not make me feel better when Jean-René chimed, "No, it's not like Paris, *either*." *Dios mio.* Where does she find them?

East St. Louis is sorta like a country Lower East Side where everybody is black and speaks English. That said, there's more neon to it, more fluid capital, *turistas,* and the velvet decor, gilded with fake gold that recently paroled felons find pleasing. We heard some Bobby "Blue" Bland music blasting out of this place callt Nasty's: we decided that was the spot.

Well, Granville insists he lead the way. "Lollie and I have been here many times," he says. We step through the most Puerto Rican doors I've seen since Ohio, into a blockade of the biggest men outside, oh, Port Arthur, Texas. There we are patted down, Granville first. "But, you know me, I'm Lollie's fiancé." There is a loud echoing shout. "You seen Lollie in here tonight?" Then, there's a return volley, "Lollie ain't been here, Lollie ain't been here." The guy who is now searching Thayer's guitar for a trigger and clips says, "Lollie ain't here. I'll need some I.D." Well, since I'd decided to carry two cameras and a case, my Konica became possible explosives or the cover for grams and ounces of what was not my right to take into Nasty's cause in Nasty's they reserve the right to serve. *Tu m'entiendes?* Finally we all get in there and get something to drink. These chicks, pretty hippy naked women, are flying up and down these poles, others are standin' over our drinks wrigglin' and writhin' so, some pussy musta been in one of my drinks. But see, I didn't get excited until Thayer took over the rhythm section of the sampler and Sawyer with his nonmaterial behind started feelin' up the naked dancers and runnin' his tongue over their nipples. Then I couldn't just enjoy myself. I got to work. Apparently Jean-René is an exhibitionist cause he got almost naked, *en realidad,* up on the bar with one of those whores. But that was after Sawyer'd filled his nose with powder of great value. I saw what Lollie liked so much in Granville, finally. He kept to himself, enjoyed everybody and danced his junkanoo whenever he felt like. That was usually after a short visit from our boy Sawyer, too. So a fine time was had by all, including the ghost of Sawyer Malveaux. If you look closely at one of the images I have of Granville and Jean-René dancing on the bar with the same woman, you'll see Sawyer's handsome head between her legs. A very nasty boy, *sí.*

But what really tickled me? I split from the group when Jean-René started playin' mazurkas at Nasty's, see. I'm walkin' like I do everywhere and who do I come upon but Lili and her gang in pursuit of some rather corporal night phantoms, a.k.a. hardened con men. Here's Rose Lynne with her leg demurely wrapped around some would-be Kid Chocolate leanin' gainst a empty storefront. Next, Bernadette sittin' on a curb, with her head under some niggah's armpit. And you know who I'm lookin' for. But Lollie is busy with Roxie's spirit, wonderin' is she up to all this marriage mess? I keep lookin'. I don't give up easy, you know that, too. At last I can take it easy. Lili and Hyacinthe are singin' doo-wop songs with Sawyer under a streetlight. *Que típica!*

Now, the wedding. How about the March on Washington all dressed up and squeezed into a church moved intact from Turin? Awright. Awright. I'm kiddin', yet there was somethin' more than spectacular about Lollie's wedding. I felt as if, and

I am not really a part of all this, but I felt as if all the years of yearning and struggling that Lili and Lollie's people had known were streaming from Lollie's pores. Lollie, of all people, the tart, the a-intellectual, the sentient, was more beautiful than anyone I'd ever know. At that moment, Lollie was even more lovely than my Liliane. And Granville, who's not my favorite brother, became before my very eyes the determination of every Moroon, Garveyite, Panther, Zapatista with the grace of Puente, Moré, and Sparrow. Maybe it's the solemnity of it all. The decision to continue *la raza* on purpose, for ourselves, not for profit. *Tu m'entiendes?* Lollie, with her dress of a thousand mantillas and pearls. Granville with his own imported Anglican priest. *Quien sabe?* The Lord, and S/he is *uno de nosotros,* moves in *maneras increíble, sí? Mi Mami,* she always told me that we never know who the spirits hold sacred. Motto: Every *negrito* soul you ever meet is precious. *Claro, que si.* Oh I'm gettin' misty-eyed and I haven't finished yet. I took a shot of Lollie and Granville lighting a holy candle that forced the mist out of my eyes and down my face like anyone's tears in the presence of the divine.

I was shaken up after the service, so I wasn't focusing, but I couldn't miss Liliane comin' toward me; her mother, Bliss, runnin' behind her, a blur, a rush of wanton energy. Liliane a vision of calm and power; *éblouissante,* as Jean-René would say, of the confusion whirling about Bliss and the new husband, barely in the frame. *N'importa.*

*N'importa porque,* we have a party to go to now. The entire wedding has turned into a *bomba* with a southern drawl, a *merengue* with Mississippi improvisation capacity. The jump-up hitched on to a get-down blues. And Lollie and Granville parade the future of the race in their loose-hipped wedding beguine. And we are all here. Lollie, Granville, Rose Lynne and her East St. Louis fling; Hyacinthe and her songs; Bernadette and the Caribbean suitor learning her ways; Thayer with the catch of the day; Jean-René with his eyes all over Bernadette, and Roxie in the diaphanous gown of our memory; Sawyer in our souls as constant resistance to the end of our celebration.

"Victor-Jésus María, you bettah bring your black ass over here and get in this picture!" I bet you can't guess who said that?

"Victor-Jésus María. Did you hear me?"

I've got to put my camera on autoset. Liliane has her mind made up.

"That's absolutely right, *cariño.* There's no room for voyeurism here. Wow. Victor, do you know you are dancin' there right next to Machito. And *La Virgen de Caridad* is romping with Sierra. Walter Rodney is sharing a rum punch with Granville and Sawyer. Oh Lord, Augusta Savage is offering Roxie a canapé. Aw. We'd love to take some more photos for you, but we've gotta be in this dance. With all our friends, our ghosts, and the gods we love.

"But, *querido,* I promise to paint it for you. . . . Okay?"